Maigret

'I love reading Simenon. He makes me think of Chekhov'
— William Faulkner

'A truly wonderful writer . . . marvellously readable – lucid, simple, absolutely in tune with the world he creates'
— Muriel Spark

'Few writers have ever conveyed with such a sure touch, the bleakness of human life'   — A. N. Wilson

'One of the greatest writers of the twentieth century . . . Simenon was unequalled at making us look inside, though the ability was masked by his brilliance at absorbing us obsessively in his stories'   — *Guardian*

'A novelist who entered his fictional world as if he were part of it'   — Peter Ackroyd

'The greatest of all, the most genuine novelist we have had in literature'   — André Gide

'Superb . . . The most addictive of writers . . . A unique teller of tales'   — *Observer*

'The mysteries of the human personality are revealed in all their disconcerting complexity'   — Anita Brookner

'A writer who, more than any other crime novelist, combined a high literary reputation with popular appeal'   — P. D. James

'A supreme writer . . . Unforgettable vividness' — *Independent*

'Compelling, remorseless, brilliant'   — John Gray

'Extraordinary masterpieces of the twentieth century'
— John Banville

GEORGES SIMENON

Maigret

Translated by ROS SCHWARTZ

PENGUIN BOOKS

PENGUIN CLASSICS

UK | USA | Canada | Ireland | Australia
India | New Zealand | South Africa

Penguin Books is part of the Penguin Random House group of companies
whose addresses can be found at global.penguinrandomhouse.com.

Penguin
Random House
UK

First published in French in *Le Jour*, in instalments from 20 February to 15 March 1934
First published in book form by Fayard 1934
This translation first published 2015

013

Set in Dante MT Std 12.5/15pt
Typeset by Palimpsest Book Production Limited, Falkirk, Stirlingshire
Printed and bound in Great Britain by Clays Ltd, Elcograf S.p.A.

A CIP catalogue record for this book is available from the British Library

ISBN: 978-0-141-39704-7

www.greenpenguin.co.uk

MIX
Paper from
responsible sources
FSC   FSC® C018179
www.fsc.org

Penguin Random House is committed to a
sustainable future for our business, our readers
and our planet. This book is made from Forest
Stewardship Council® certified paper.

Maigret

1.

Maigret struggled to open his eyes, frowning, as if distrustful of the voice that had just shouted at him, dragging him out of a deep sleep:

'Uncle!'

His eyes still closed, he sighed, groped at the sheet and realized that this was no dream, that something was the matter, because his hand had not encountered Madame Maigret's warm body where it should have been.

Finally he opened his eyes. It was a clear night. Madame Maigret, standing by the leaded window, was pulling back the curtain while downstairs someone was banging on the door and the noise reverberated throughout the house.

'Uncle! It's me!'

Madame Maigret was still looking out. Her hair wound in curling pins gave her a strange halo.

'It's Philippe,' she said, knowing full well that Maigret was awake and that he was turned towards her, waiting. 'Are you going to get up?'

Maigret went downstairs first, barefoot in his felt slippers. He had hastily pulled on a pair of trousers and shrugged on his jacket as he descended the staircase. At the eighth stair, he had to duck to avoid hitting his head on the beam. He usually did so automatically, but this time he forgot and banged his forehead. He groaned and swore as he reached the freezing hall. He went into the kitchen, which was a little warmer.

There were iron bars across the door. On the other side, Philippe was saying to someone:

'I won't be long. We'll be in Paris before daylight.'

Madame Maigret could be heard padding around upstairs. Maigret pulled open the door, surly from the knock he had just given himself.

'It's you!' he muttered, seeing his nephew standing in the road.

A huge moon floated above the leafless poplars, making the sky so light that the tiniest branches were silhouetted against it while, beyond the bend, the Loire was a glittering swarm of silvery spangles.

'East wind!' thought Maigret mechanically, as would any local on seeing the surface of the river whipped up.

It is one of those country habits, as is standing in the doorway without saying anything, looking at the intruder and waiting for him to speak.

'I hope I haven't woken Aunt up, at least?'

Philippe's face was frozen stiff. Behind him the shape of a G7 taxi stood out incongruously against the white-frosted landscape.

'Are you leaving the driver outside?'

'I need to talk to you right away.'

'Come inside quickly, both of you,' called Madame Maigret from the kitchen where she was lighting an oil lamp.

She added to her nephew:

'We haven't got electricity yet. The house has been

wired, but we're waiting to be connected to the power supply.'

A lightbulb was dangling from a flex. People notice little details like that for no reason. And when they are already on edge, it is the sort of thing that can irritate them. During the minutes that followed, Philippe's eyes kept returning to that bulb, which served no purpose other than to emphasize everything that was antiquated about this rustic house, or rather everything that is precarious about modern comforts.

'Have you come from Paris?'

Maigret was leaning against the chimney breast, not properly awake yet. The presence of the taxi on the road made the question as redundant as the lightbulb, but sometimes people speak for the sake of saying something.

'I'm going to tell you everything, Uncle. I'm in big trouble. If you don't help me, if you don't come to Paris with me, I don't know what will become of me. I'm going out of my mind. I'm in such a state I even forgot to give my aunt a kiss.'

Madame Maigret stood there, having slipped a dressing gown over her nightdress. Philippe's lips brushed her cheek three times, performing the ritual like a child. Then he sat down at the table, clutching his head in his hands.

Maigret filled his pipe as he watched him, while his wife stacked twigs in the fireplace. There was something strange in the air, something threatening. Since Maigret had retired, he had lost the habit of getting up in the middle of the night and he couldn't help being reminded of nights spent beside a sick person or a dead body.

'I don't know how I could have been so stupid!' Philippe suddenly sobbed.

He poured out his tale of woe in a sudden rush, punctuated by hiccups. He looked about him like a person seeking to pin his agitation on something, while, in contrast to this outburst of emotion, Maigret turned up the wick of the oil lamp and the first flames leapt up from the fireplace.

'First of all, you're going to drink something.'

The uncle took a bottle of brandy and two glasses from a cupboard that contained some leftover food and smelled of cold meat. Madame Maigret put on her clogs to go and fetch some logs from the woodshed.

'To your good health! Now try to calm down.'

The smell of burning twigs mingled with that of the brandy. Philippe, dazed, watched his aunt loom silently out of the darkness, her arms filled with logs.

He was short-sighted and, seen from a certain angle, his eyes looked enormous behind his spectacle lenses, giving him the appearance of a frightened child.

'It happened last night. I was supposed to be on a stake-out in Rue Fontaine—'

'Just a moment,' interrupted Maigret, sitting astride a straw-bottomed chair and lighting his pipe. 'Who are you working with?'

'With Chief Inspector Amadieu.'

'Go on.'

Drawing gently on his pipe, Maigret narrowed his eyes and stared at the lime-plastered wall and the shelf with copper saucepans, caressing the images that were so familiar to him. At Quai des Orfèvres, Amadieu's office was the last one on the left at the end of the corridor. Amadieu himself was a skinny, sad man who had been promoted to divisional chief when Maigret had retired.

'Does he still have a drooping moustache?'

'Yes. Yesterday we had a summons for Pepito Palestrino, the owner of the Floria, in Rue Fontaine.'

'What number?'

'Fifty-three, next to the optician.'

'In my day, that was the Toréador. Cocaine dealing?'

'Cocaine initially. Then something else too. The chief had heard rumours that Pepito was mixed up in the Barnabé job, the guy who was shot in Place Blanche a fortnight ago. You must have read about it in the papers.'

'Make us some coffee!' said Maigret to his wife.

And, with the relieved sigh of a dog who finally settles down after chasing its tail, he leaned his elbows on the back of his chair and rested his chin on his folded hands. From time to time, Philippe removed his glasses to wipe the lenses and, for a few moments, he appeared to be blind. He was a tall, plump, auburn-haired boy with baby-pink skin.

'You know that we can no longer do as we please. In your day, no one would have batted an eyelid at arresting Pepito in the middle of the night. But now, we have to keep to the letter of the law. That's why the chief decided to carry out the arrest at eight o'clock in the morning. In the meantime, it was my job to keep an eye on the fellow . . .'

He was getting bogged down in the dense quiet of the room, then, with a start, he remembered his predicament and cast around helplessly.

For Maigret, the few words spoken by his nephew exuded the whiff of Paris. He could picture the Floria's neon sign, the doorman on the alert for cars arriving, and his nephew turning up in the neighbourhood that night.

'Take off your overcoat, Philippe,' interrupted Madame Maigret. 'You'll catch cold when you go outside.'

He was wearing a dinner-jacket. It looked quite incongruous in the low-ceilinged kitchen with its heavy beams and red-tiled floor.

'Have another drink—'

But in a fresh outburst of anger Philippe jumped up, wringing his hands violently enough to crush his bones.

'If only you knew, Uncle—'

He was on the verge of tears, his eyes stayed dry. His gaze fell on the electric lightbulb again. He stamped his foot.

'I bet I'll be arrested later!'

Madame Maigret, who was pouring boiling water over the coffee, turned around, saucepan in hand.

'What on earth are you talking about?'

And Maigret, still puffing on his pipe, opened his night-shirt collar with its delicate red embroidery.

'So you were on a stakeout opposite the Floria—'

'Not opposite. I went inside,' said Philippe, still on his feet. 'At the back of the club there's a little office where Pepito has set up a camp bed. That's where he usually sleeps after closing up the joint.'

A cart rumbled past on the road. The clock had stopped. Maigret glanced at his watch hanging from a nail above the fireplace. The hands showed half past four. In the

cowsheds, milking had begun and carts were trundling to
Orléans market. The taxi was still waiting outside the
house.

'I wanted to be clever,' confessed Philippe. 'Last week
the chief yelled at me and told me—'

He turned red and trailed off, trying to fix his gaze on
something.

'He told you—?'

'I can't remember—'

'Well I can! If it's Amadieu, he probably came out with
something along the lines of: "You're a maverick, young
man, a maverick like your uncle!"'

Philippe said neither yes nor no.

'Anyway, I wanted to be clever,' he hastily went on.
'When the customers left, at around 1.30, I hid in the toilet.
I thought that if Pepito had got wind of anything, he might
try and get rid of the stuff. And do you know what happened?'

Maigret, more solemn now, slowly shook his head.

'Pepito was alone. Of that I'm certain! Suddenly, there
was a gunshot. It took a few moments for it to dawn on
me, then it took me a few more moments to run into the
bar. It looked bigger, at night. It was lit by a single lightbulb. Pepito was lying between two rows of tables and as
he fell he'd knocked over some chairs. He was dead.'

Maigret rose and poured himself another glassful of
brandy, while his wife signalled to him not to drink too
much.

'Is that all?'

Philippe was pacing up and down. And this young man,

9

who generally had difficulty expressing himself, began to wax eloquent in a dry, bitter tone.

'No, that's not all! That's when I did something really stupid! I was scared. I couldn't think straight. The empty bar was sinister, it felt as if it was shrouded in greyness. There were streamers strewn on the floor and over the tables. Pepito was lying in a strange position, on his side, his hand close to his wound, and he seemed to be looking at me. What can I say? I took out my revolver and I started talking. I yelled out some nonsense and my voice scared me even more. There were shadowy corners everywhere, drapes, and I had the impression they were moving. I pulled myself together and went over to have a look. I flung open a door and yanked down a velvet curtain. I found the switchbox and I wanted to turn on the lights. I pushed the switches at random. And that was even more frightening. A red projector lit the place up. Fans started humming in every corner. "Who's there?" I shouted again.'

He bit his lip. His aunt looked at him, as distressed as he was. He was her sister's son and had been born in Alsace. Maigret had wangled him a job at police headquarters.

'I'd feel happier knowing he was in the civil service,' his mother had said.

And now, he panted:

'Please don't be angry with me, Uncle. I don't know myself how it happened. I can barely remember. In any case, I fired a shot, because I thought I saw something move. I rushed forwards and then stopped. I thought I heard footsteps, whisperings. But there was nothing but emptiness. I would never have believed the place was so big and full of obstacles. In the end, I found myself in the office. There was a gun on the table. I grabbed it without thinking. The barrel was still warm. I took out the chamber and saw that there was one bullet missing.'

'Idiot!' groaned Maigret between clenched teeth.

The coffee was steaming and Madame Maigret, sugar bowl in hand, stood there not knowing what she was doing.

'I had completely lost my mind. I still thought I could hear a noise over by the door. I ran. It was only later that I realized I had a gun in each hand.'

'Where did you put the gun?'

Maigret's tone was harsh. Philippe stared at the floor.

'All sorts of things were going through my mind. If it was a murder, people would think that since I'd been alone with Pepito—'

'Dear God!' groaned Madame Maigret.

'It only lasted for a few seconds. I put the gun near Pepito's hand, to make it look like a suicide, then—'

Maigret rose to his feet and took up his favourite position in front of the fireplace, his hands clasped behind his back. He was unshaven. He had put on a little weight since the days when he used to stand like that in front of his stove at Quai des Orfèvres.

'When you left, you ran into someone, am I right?'

He knew it.

'Just as I was closing the door behind me, I bumped into a man who was walking past. I apologized. Our faces were almost touching. I don't even know whether after that I closed the door properly. I walked to Place Clichy. I took a taxi and gave the driver your address.'

Madame Maigret put the sugar bowl down on the beech table and slowly asked her husband:

'Which suit are you wearing?'

For half an hour, it was a mad rush.

Maigret could be heard shaving and getting dressed in the bedroom. Madame Maigret cooked some eggs and questioned Philippe.

'Have you heard from your mother?'

'She's well. She was planning to come to Paris for Easter.'

The driver was invited in, but he refused to remove his heavy brown overcoat. Droplets of water trembled in his moustache. He sat down in a corner and stayed put.

'My braces?' shouted Maigret from upstairs.

'In the top drawer.'

Maigret came down wearing his coat with a velvet collar and his bowler hat. He pushed away the eggs waiting for him on the table and, defying his wife, drank a fourth glass of brandy.

It was 5.30 when the door opened and the three men stepped outside and got into the taxi. It took a while for the engine to start. Madame Maigret stood shivering in the doorway while the oil lamp made the reddish reflections dance on the little window panes.

The sky was so light, it felt like daybreak. But this was February and it was the night itself that was silver-coloured. Each blade of grass was rimed with frost. The apple trees in the neighbouring orchard were iced so white that they looked as fragile as spun glass.

'See you in two or three days!' yelled Maigret.

Philippe, embarrassed, shouted:

'Goodbye, Aunt!'

The driver slammed the car door again and crunched the gears for a moment.

'Please forgive me, Uncle —'

'What for?'

What for? Philippe didn't dare say. He was asking forgiveness because there was something dramatic about this departure. He recalled his uncle's silhouette earlier, by the fireplace, with his nightshirt, his old clothes, his slippers.

And now, he barely dared look at him. It was indeed Maigret who was beside him, smoking his pipe, his velvet collar upturned, his hat perched on his head. But it wasn't an enthusiastic Maigret. It wasn't even a Maigret who was sure of himself. Twice he turned round and watched his little house receding.

'Did you say that Amadieu will arrive at Rue Fontaine at eight?' he asked.

'Yes, at eight o'clock.'

They had time. The taxi was going quite fast. They drove through Orléans, where the first trams were setting out. Less than an hour later, they reached the market in Arpajon.

'What do you think, Uncle?'

It was draughty in the back of the car. The sky was clear. There was a golden glow in the east.

'How could Pepito have been killed?' sighed Philippe, who received no reply.

They stopped after Arpajon to warm up in a café and almost at once it was daylight, with a pale sun slowly rising where the fields met the horizon.

'There was no one but him and me in—'

'Be quiet!' said Maigret wearily.

His nephew huddled in his corner with the look of a child caught misbehaving, not daring to take his eyes off the door.

They entered Paris as the early-morning bustle was beginning. Past the Lion de Belfort, Boulevard Raspail, the Pont-Neuf . . .

The city looked as if it had been washed in clean water, so bright were the colours. A train of barges was gliding slowly up the Seine and the tugboat whistled, puffing out clouds of immaculate steam to announce its flotilla.

'How many passers-by were there in Rue Fontaine when you came out?'

'I only saw the man I ran into.'

Maigret sighed and emptied his pipe, tapping it against his heel.

The driver pulled down the glass partition and inquired: 'Where to?'

They stopped for a moment at a hotel on the embankment to drop off Maigret's suitcase, then they got back into the taxi and made their way to Rue Fontaine.

'It's not so much what happened at the Floria that worries me. It's the man who bumped into you.'

'What are you thinking?'

'I'm not thinking anything!'

He came out with this favourite expression from the past as he turned round to glimpse the outline, once so familiar, of the Palais de Justice.

'At one point I thought of going to the big chief and telling him the whole story,' muttered Philippe.

Maigret did not answer and, until they reached Rue Fontaine, he kept his gaze fixed on the view of the Seine as it flowed through a fine blue and gold mist.

They pulled up a hundred metres from number 53. Philippe turned up the collar of his overcoat to conceal his dinner-jacket, but at the sight of his patent-leather shoes, people turned round to stare all the same.

It was only 6.50. A window-cleaner was washing the windows of the corner café, the Tabac Fontaine, which stayed open all night. People on their way to work stopped off for a quick *café crème* with a croissant. There was only a waiter serving since the owner did not get to bed before five or six in the morning and rose at midday. He was a swarthy young southern-looking fellow with black hair. There were cigar ends and cigarette butts lying on a table next to a slate used for keeping score for card games.

Maigret bought a packet of shag and ordered a sandwich, while Philippe grew impatient.

'What happened last night?' asked Maigret, his mouth full of bread and ham.

And, gathering up the change, the waiter answered bluntly:

'People are saying the owner of the Floria was killed.'

'Palestrino?'

'I don't know. I'm on the day shift. And during the day, we don't have anything to do with the nightclubs.'

They left. Philippe did not dare say anything.

'You see?' grumbled Maigret.

Standing on the kerb, he added:

'That's the work of the man you bumped into, you realize.

Theoretically, no one should know anything before eight o'clock.'

They walked towards the Floria, but they stopped fifty metres short. They spotted the peaked cap of a Paris police sergeant standing in front of the door. On the opposite pavement, a knot of people had gathered.

'What shall I do?'

'Your chief is bound to be at the scene. Go up to him and tell him—'

'What about you, Uncle?'

Maigret shrugged and went on:

'—Tell him the truth.'

'Supposing he asks where I went next?'

'Tell him you came to fetch me.'

There was resignation in his voice. They had got off on the wrong foot, and that was all! It was a stupid business and Maigret felt like gnashing his teeth.

'I'm sorry, Uncle!'

'No emotional scenes in the street! If they let you go free, meet me in the Chope du Pont-Neuf. If I'm not there, I'll leave you a note.'

They did not even shake hands. Philippe headed straight for the Floria. The sergeant did not know him and tried to bar him from entering. Philippe had to show his badge, then he vanished inside.

Maigret remained at a distance, his hands in his pockets, like the other onlookers. He waited. He waited for almost half an hour, without the least idea of what was going on inside the club.

Detective Chief Inspector Amadieu came out first,

followed by a short, nondescript man who looked like a waiter.

And Maigret needed no explanations. He knew that this was the man who had bumped into Philippe. He could guess Amadieu's question.

'Was it right here that you bumped into him?'

The man nodded. Inspector Amadieu beckoned Philippe, who was still inside. He came out, looking as nervous as a young musician, as if the entire street were aware of the suspicions that were about to engulf him.

'And was this the gentleman who was coming out at that moment?' Amadieu must have been saying, tugging his brown moustache.

The man nodded again.

There were two other police officers. The divisional chief glanced at his watch and, after a brief discussion, the man sauntered off and went into the Tabac Fontaine while the policemen went back inside the Floria.

Fifteen minutes later, two cars arrived. It was the public prosecutor.

'I've got to go back to repeat my statement,' the man from the Floria told the waiter at the Tabac Fontaine. 'Another white wine and Vichy, quick!'

And, discomfited by Maigret's insistent stare as he stood nearby drinking a beer, he lowered his voice and asked:

'Who's that?'

2.

Maigret sat with his head bent over his work with the application of a schoolboy. He drew a rectangle and placed a little cross somewhere in the centre. Then he stared at his effort and frowned. The rectangle represented the Floria, and the cross, Pepito. At the far end of the rectangle, Maigret drew another, smaller one: the office. And in this office he placed a dot indicating the gun.

This was pointless. It meant nothing. The case wasn't a geometry problem. Maigret doggedly continued all the same, scrunched the page into a ball and started all over again on a fresh sheet.

Only now he was no longer concerned with placing crosses in rectangles. Poring over the page, deeply engrossed, he tried to pin down a snatch of conversation, a look, an unwitting attitude.

He sat alone at his former table at the back of the Chope du Pont-Neuf. And it was too late to wonder whether he had been right or wrong to come. Everyone had seen him. The owner had shaken his hand.

'How's it going with the chickens and rabbits?'

Maigret was sitting by the window and he could see the Pont-Neuf bathed in a rosy glow, the steps of the Palais de Justice, the gates of the police headquarters. A white napkin under his arm, the beaming owner was in a chatty mood:

'So life's good! Dropping in to see your old pals?'

The beat officers were still in the habit of playing a hand of *belote* in the Chope before setting off on their rounds. There were some new faces who didn't know Maigret, but the others, after greeting Maigret, spoke to their colleagues in hushed tones.

That was when he had drawn his first rectangle, his first cross. The hours dragged by. At aperitif time, there were a dozen 'boys' in the place.

Trusty Lucas, who had worked with Maigret on a hundred cases, came over looking slightly sheepish.

'How are you, chief? Come for a breath of Paris air?' Lucas still called him chief, in memory of the old days.

And Maigret, between two puffs of smoke, merely muttered:

'What did Amadieu have to say?'

There was no point lying to him. He could see their faces and he knew the Police Judiciaire well enough to know what was going on. It was midday, and Philippe had not yet put in an appearance at the Chope.

'You know what Inspector Amadieu is like. We've had a few problems at HQ recently. Things are a bit tricky with the public prosecutor. So—'

'What did he say?'

'That you were here, of course. That you were going to try to—'

'Let me guess. His words were "act the wise guy".'

'I have to go,' stammered Lucas, embarrassed.

Maigret ordered another beer and became absorbed in

19

drawing his rectangles while most of the tables were talking about him.

He ate lunch at the same table, now in the sunlight. The photographer from the criminal records office was eating nearby. As he drank his coffee, Maigret repeated to himself, pencil in hand:

'Pepito was here, between two rows of tables. The murderer was concealed somewhere. There's no shortage of hiding places. He fired, unaware of the presence of that idiot Philippe, then went into the office to get something. He had just put his gun down on the desk when he heard a noise and so he hid again. And from then on, the two of them played cat and mouse.'

It was simple. Pointless looking for any other explanation. The murderer had eventually reached the door without being seen and made it out into the street while Philippe was still inside.

So far, nothing extraordinary. Any fool would have done the same thing. The clever part was what happened next: the idea of ensuring that someone would recognize Philippe and testify against him.

And, a few moments later, it was done. The murderer had found his man, in an empty street in the dead of night. This person bumped into Philippe as he emerged and rushed off to fetch the policeman on duty in Place Blanche.

'I say, officer, I've just seen a suspicious-looking character coming out of the Floria. He was in such a rush that he didn't bother to close the door.'

Maigret, without looking at his former colleagues, who

were drinking beers, could guess what the old-timers were whispering to the new boys:

'Have you heard of Detective Chief Inspector Maigret? That's him!'

Amadieu, who didn't like him, must have announced in the corridors of the Police Judiciaire:

'He's going to try and act the wise guy. But we'll show him!'

It was four in the afternoon and Philippe had not appeared yet. The newspapers came off the presses with details of the murder, including his alleged confession. Another dirty trick of Amadieu's.

Quai des Orfèvres was in turmoil, phones ringing, files dredged up, witnesses and informers brought in for questioning.

Maigret's nostrils were quivering as he sat hunched on the banquette patiently doing little drawings with the tip of his pencil.

He had to find Pepito's killer at all costs. But he was not on good form, he felt afraid, anxious as to whether he would succeed. He watched the young police officers and tried to fathom what they thought of him.

Philippe did not arrive until 5.45. He stood there for a moment, as if dazzled by the light. As he sat down beside Maigret, he attempted a smile and stammered:

'It went on for ages!'

He was so exhausted that he wiped his hand across his brow as if to collect his thoughts.

'I've been at the prosecutor's office. The examining magistrate questioned me for an hour and a half. But before that, he made me wait in the corridor for two hours.'

Everyone was watching them. And while Philippe talked, Maigret looked at the men facing them.

'You know, Uncle, it's much more serious than we thought.'

For Maigret, each word was loaded with significance. He knew the examining magistrate, Gastambide, a stocky Basque who was meticulous and contemptuous, who weighed up his words, spent several minutes formulating his sentences then letting them drop as if to declare:

'What can you say to that?'

And Maigret was familiar with that corridor, filled with defendants under police guard, the benches crammed with restless witnesses, women in tears. If Philippe had been made to wait, it was deliberate.

'The magistrate told me not to deal with any cases, to take no action before the end of the investigation. I am to consider myself suspended from duty and I must remain at his disposal.'

It was aperitif hour, the noisiest time at the Chope du Pont-Neuf. All the tables were full. The air was thick with pipe and cigarette smoke. From time to time, a newcomer greeted Maigret from across the room.

Philippe did not dare look at anyone, not even his companion.

'I'm very sorry, Uncle.'

'What else has happened?'

'Everyone thought, naturally, that the Floria would be closed, at least for a few days. But it isn't going to be. Today, there was a series of phone calls, some baffling developments. Apparently, the Floria was sold two days ago and

Pepito was no longer the owner. The buyer has friends in high places and tonight the joint will be open for business as usual.'

Maigret frowned. Was it because of what he had just heard, or because Detective Chief Inspector Amadieu had just walked in with a colleague and sat down at the other end of the room?

'Godet!' Maigret shouted.

Godet was an inspector from the vice squad who was playing cards three tables away. He turned round, cards in hand, unsure whether to get up.

'When you've finished your game!'

And Maigret screwed up all his scraps of paper and threw them on to the floor. He downed his beer in one gulp and wiped his mouth, looking over in Amadieu's direction.

Amadieu had heard him. He watched the scene from a distance as he poured water into his Pernod. Intrigued, Godet finally went over to Maigret's table.

'Did you want to speak to me, sir?'

'Hello, old friend!' said Maigret, shaking his hand. 'A simple piece of information. Are you still with the Vice? Good. Can you tell me whether Cageot showed his face at HQ this morning?'

'Hold on. I think he came into the office at around eleven.'

'Thank you, my friend.'

That was all! Maigret looked at Amadieu. Amadieu looked at Maigret. And now it was Amadieu who was uncomfortable and Maigret was the one suppressing a smile.

Philippe did not dare speak. The case had just moved up a rung. The game was being played over his head and he didn't even know the rules.

'Godet!' bawled a voice.

This time, all the police officers in the room shuddered as they watched the inspector get up again, still holding his cards, and walk over to Chief Inspector Amadieu.

There was no need to hear what was said. It was clear that Amadieu wanted to know:

'What did he ask you?'

'Whether I'd seen Cageot this morning.'

Maigret lit his pipe, let the match burn down to the very end and finally rose, calling:

'Waiter!'

Drawn up to his full height, he waited for his change, glancing casually around the room.

'Where are we going?' asked Philippe once they were outside.

Maigret turned to him, as if surprised to see him there.

'You're going to bed,' he said.

'What about you, Uncle?'

Maigret shrugged, thrust his hands in his pockets and walked off without answering. He had just spent one of the most unpleasant days of his life. Hours on end stuck in his corner. He had felt old and feeble, with no energy, no inspiration.

Then the shift happened. A little flame shot up. But he had to take advantage of it right away.

'We'll see, damn it!' he grunted to boost his spirits.

Normally, at this hour, he would be reading his

newspaper under the lamp, his legs outstretched in front of the log fire.

'Do you come to Paris often?'

Maigret, propping up the bar of the Floria, shook his head and merely replied:

'Uh-huh, from time to time . . .'

He was feeling buoyant again. He did not express his good humour in smiles, but he had an inner feeling of well-being. One of his gifts was the ability to laugh inwardly without betraying his outer gravitas. A woman was sitting next to him. She asked him to buy her a drink and he nodded in acquiescence.

Two years ago, a prostitute would never have made that mistake. But his overcoat with its velvet collar and his standard black, hard-wearing serge suit and tie told her nothing. If she mistook him for a provincial out on the town, it meant he had changed.

'Something happened here, didn't it?' he muttered.

'The boss got bumped off last night.'

She also misread the look in his eye, which she thought was one of interest. But things were not so straightforward! Maigret was back in a world he had long since left behind. This nondescript little woman, he knew her without knowing her. He was certain that she did not have a record and that, on her passport, her occupation was given as *artiste* or *dancer*. As for the Chinese barman who served them, Maigret could have recited his criminal history. The cloakroom attendant, on the other hand, had clocked him and had greeted him anxiously, trying to place him.

Among the waiters, there were at least two whom Maigret had brought into his office in the past for questioning in cases similar to Pepito's killing.

He ordered a brandy with water. He vaguely watched the room and instinctively positioned crosses, as he had done on paper. Customers who had read the papers were asking questions and the waiters were explaining, pointing out the spot near the fifth table where the body had been found.

'Would you like to share a bottle of champagne?'

'No, dear.'

The woman almost guessed, and was at least intrigued as Maigret's gaze followed the new owner, a young man with fair hair whom he had known as the manager of a Montparnasse dance hall.

'Will you see me home?'

'Of course! In a while.'

In the meantime, he went into the toilets and guessed where Philippe had hidden. At the back of the main room, he could glimpse the office with its door ajar. But that was of no interest. He knew the scenario before setting foot in Rue Fontaine. The actors too. Going round the room, he could point to each person, saying:

'At this table, we have a newlywed couple from the South out for a night on the town. This young man who is already drunk is a young German who will end the night minus his wallet. Over there, the gigolo with a criminal record and packets of cocaine in his pockets. He is in cahoots with the head waiter, who has done three years inside. The plump brunette spent ten years at Maxim's and is winding up her career in Montmartre—'

He returned to the bar.

'Can I have another cocktail?' asked the woman, for whom he had already bought a drink.

'What's your name?'

'Fernande.'

'What were you doing last night?'

'I was with three young men, boys from good families, who wanted to take ether. I went with them to a hotel in Rue Notre-Dame-de-Lorette.'

Maigret did not smile, but he could have continued the story for her.

'First, we went into the pharmacy in Rue Montmartre separately and bought a little bottle of ether each. I wasn't entirely sure what was going to happen. We got undressed. But they didn't even look at me. All four of us lay down on the bed. When they inhaled the ether, one got up and said in this strange voice: "Oh! There are angels on top of the wardrobe . . . Aren't they lovely . . . I'm going to catch them . . ." He tried to get up and fell on to the rug. Me, the smell made me feel sick. I asked them if that was all they wanted from me and I got dressed again. But I did laugh. There was a bug on the pillow between two of their heads, and I can still hear the voice of one of the boys saying, as if in a dream: "There's a bug in front of my face!" "And mine!" sighed the other one. And they didn't budge. They were both squinting.'

She downed her drink in one go, and decreed:

'Barmy!'

All the same, she was starting to grow anxious.

'You're keeping me for the night, aren't you?'

'Of course! Of course!' replied Maigret.

There was a curtain dividing the bar from the lobby where the cloakroom was. From his seat, Maigret could see through the slit in the curtain. Suddenly he jumped down from his stool and took a few steps. A man had just walked in, and said to the cloakroom attendant:

'Nothing new?'

'Good evening, Monsieur Cageot!'

It was Maigret speaking, his hands in his jacket pockets, his pipe in his mouth. The man he was addressing, who had his back to him, slowly turned around, looked him up and down, and grunted:

'So you're here!'

The red curtain and the music were behind them, and in front of them the door opened on to the cold street where the doorman was pacing up and down. Cageot was reluctant to take off his overcoat.

Fernande, feeling uneasy, poked her nose out, but withdrew immediately.

'Will you have a drink?'

Cageot had finally made up his mind and handed his overcoat to the cloakroom attendant, watching Maigret all the while.

'If you like,' he agreed.

The head waiter hurried over to show them to a free table. Without looking at the wine list, the newcomer muttered:

'Mumm 26!'

He was not in evening dress, but was wearing a dark-grey suit as ill-fitting as Maigret's. He was not even freshly shaven and a greyish stubble ate into his cheeks.

'I thought you'd retired?'

'So did I!'

This seemed pretty innocuous, yet Cageot frowned, and signalled to the girl selling cigars and cigarettes. Fernande sat at the bar, wide-eyed. And young Albert, who was playing the part of the owner, wondered whether or not he should go over to them.

'Cigar?'

'No thank you,' said Maigret, emptying his pipe.

'Are you in Paris for long?'

'Until Pepito's killer is behind bars.'

They did not raise their voices. Next to them, high-spirited men in dinner-jackets were pelting each other with cotton-wool balls and throwing paper streamers. The saxophonist wandered solemnly from table to table playing his instrument.

'Have they called you back to investigate this case?'

Germain Cageot had a long, lifeless face and bushy eyebrows the colour of grey mould. He was the last man one would expect to meet in a place where people go to have fun. He spoke slowly, frostily, gauging the effect of each word.

'I came of my own accord,' Maigret replied.

'Are you working for yourself?'

'One could say that.'

It seemed unimportant. Fernande herself must have been thinking that it was pure chance that her companion knew Cageot.

'How long ago did you buy the place?'

'The Floria? You're mistaken. It belongs to Albert.'

'As it did Pepito.'

Cageot did not deny it, but merely smiled mirthlessly and stopped the waiter who was about to pour him some champagne.

'What else?' he asked in the tone of someone casting around for a topic of conversation.

'What's your alibi?'

Cageot gave another smile, even more neutral, and reeled off without batting an eyelid:

'I went to bed at nine as I had a touch of flu. The concierge brought me up a hot toddy and gave it to me in bed.'

Neither of them paid any attention to the hubbub that surrounded them like a wall. They were used to it. Maigret smoked his pipe, and Cageot a cigar.

'Still drinking Pougues mineral water?' asked the former chief inspector as Cageot poured him a glass of champagne.

'Still.'

They sat facing each other, grave and slightly sullen like two soothsayers. At a neighbouring table, some woman who didn't know better was aiming cotton-wool balls at their noses.

'You were quick to get the place re-opened!' commented Maigret between two puffs of smoke.

'I'm still pretty well connected with the "boys".'

'Are you aware that there's a kid who's stupidly compromised in this business?'

'I read something along those lines in the papers. A

young cop who was hiding in the toilet and who panicked and killed Pepito.'

The jazz band struck up again. An Englishman, all the more priggish for being drunk, brushed past Maigret murmuring:

'Excuse me.'

'Go ahead.'

And Fernande, at the bar, was watching him with a worried look. Maigret smiled at her.

'Young police officers are hot-headed,' sighed Cageot.

'That's what I said to my nephew.'

'Is your nephew interested in these matters?'

'He was the kid hiding in the toilet.'

Cageot could not turn pale, because his face was always ashen. But he took a hasty sip of mineral water, then wiped his mouth.

'That's too bad, isn't it?'

'That's exactly what I said to him.'

Fernande jerked her chin at the clock, which showed 1.30. Maigret signalled that he was coming.

'To your health,' said Cageot.

'To yours.'

'Is it pleasant, where you're living? I've heard you've moved out to the country.'

'It is pleasant, yes.'

'Winter in Paris is unhealthy.'

'I thought the same thing when I heard about Pepito's death.'

'Be my guest, please,' protested Cageot as Maigret opened his wallet.

Maigret still put fifty francs down on the table and stood up, saying:

'So long!'

He just walked past the bar and whispered to Fernande:

'Come on.'

'Have you paid?'

In the street, she wasn't sure whether to take his arm. He still had his hands in his pockets and walked with big, slow strides.

'D'you know Cageot?' she asked shyly at length, slipping into informality

'He's from my part of the world.'

'You know, you should be careful. He's a bit of a dodgy character. I'm telling you this because you seem like a good man.'

'Have you slept with him?'

Then Fernande, who had to take two steps to Maigret's every stride, replied simply:

'He doesn't sleep with anyone!'

In Meung, Madame Maigret was fast asleep in the house that smelled of wood smoke and goat's milk. In his hotel room in Rue des Dames, Philippe had finally fallen asleep too, his glasses on the bedside table.

3.

Maigret perched on the edge of the bed while Fernande, her legs crossed, gave a contented sigh as she slipped off her shoes. With the same lack of inhibition she hitched up her green silk dress to undo her garters.

'Aren't you getting undressed?'

Maigret shook his head, but she didn't notice as she was pulling her dress over her head.

Fernande had a small apartment in Rue Blanche. The red-carpeted staircase smelled of wax floor polish. There were empty milk bottles standing outside every door on the way up. Once inside the apartment, they had crossed a living room cluttered with knick-knacks and Maigret had a glimpse of a spotless kitchen where all the items were arranged with meticulous care.

'What are you thinking about?' asked Fernande as she peeled off her stockings to reveal her long, white legs and then examined her toes with interest.

'Nothing. May I smoke?'

'There are cigarettes on the table.'

Maigret paced up and down, his pipe between his teeth, and stopped in front of an enlarged portrait of a woman in her fifties, then in front of a copper pot in which a plant stood. The floor was waxed and near the door were two pieces of felt shaped like shoe soles, which Fernande must have used to walk around so as not to mark the floor.

'Are you from the North?' he asked, without looking at her.

'How can you tell?'

Finally he went over and stood in front of her. Her hair was vaguely blonde, with an auburn tinge, her features irregular – an elongated mouth, a pointed nose covered in freckles.

'I'm from Roubaix.'

You could tell from the way the apartment was arranged and polished and from the spick-and-span kitchen in particular. Maigret was sure that in the morning, Fernande sat there by the stove and drank a big bowl of coffee while she read the paper.

Now she gazed at her companion with a hint of anxiety.

'Aren't you getting undressed?' she repeated, rising and going over to the mirror.

Then, immediately suspicious:

'Why did you come?'

She sensed something was not quite right. Her mind was busy working it out.

'You're right, I didn't come for *that*,' admitted Maigret with a smile.

His grin broadened as she grabbed a bathrobe, suddenly overcome with modesty.

'So what *do* you want?'

She could not guess. Even though she was adept at categorizing men. She took in her visitor's shoes, tie and eyes.

'But you're not from the police, are you?'

'Sit down. We're going to have a nice friendly chat. You're not entirely mistaken, because I was a detective chief inspector with the Police Judiciaire for many years.'

She frowned.

'Don't be afraid. I'm not there any more! I've retired to the countryside and the reason I'm in Paris now is because Cageot's up to his old tricks.'

'So that's why!' she said under her breath as she recalled the two men sitting at the table and behaving oddly.

'I need proof, and there are people whom I can't question.'

She no longer treated him like a punter – now she addressed him formally.

'You require my help? Is that it?'

'You've guessed it. You know as well as I do, don't you, that the Floria is full of crooks and scum?'

She sighed to signal her assent.

'The real boss is Cageot, who also owns the Pélican and the Boule Verte.'

'People say he's opened a place in Nice too.'

Now they were sitting at the table facing each other, and Fernande asked:

'Would you like a hot drink?'

'Not now. You've heard about the business in Place Blanche, a couple of weeks ago. A car drove past, with three or four men inside, at around three in the morning. Between Place Blanche and Place Clichy, the door opened and one of the men was thrown out on to the road. Dead. He'd just been stabbed.'

'Barnabé!' said Fernande.

'Did you know him?'

'He used to come to the Floria.'

'Well, that was Cageot's doing. I don't know if he was in the car himself, but Pepito was with them. And last night, he copped it.'

She said nothing. She was thinking and her brow was furrowed, making her resemble an ordinary housewife.

'What's it to you?' she protested at length.

'If I don't catch Cageot, my nephew will be convicted in his place.'

'The tall redhead who looks like a tax clerk?'

Now it was Maigret's turn to be surprised.

'How do you know him?'

'He's been hanging around the bar at the Floria for the last couple of days or so. I clocked him because he didn't dance and he spoke to no one. Last night, he bought me a drink. I tried to worm some information out of him and he more or less admitted it, stammering that he couldn't tell me anything, but that he was on an important mission.'

'The fool!'

Maigret rose and got straight to the point.

'So, are we agreed? There'll be two thousand francs for you if you help me nail Cageot.'

She couldn't help smiling. She found this entertaining.

'What do I have to do?'

'First of all, I need to know whether or not Cageot showed his face in the Tabac Fontaine last night.'

'Shall I go there tonight?'

'Right away if you like.'

She shrugged off her bathrobe and, dress in hand, looked at Maigret for a moment.

'Do you really want me to put my clothes back on?'

'Yes,' he sighed, putting a hundred francs on the mantelpiece.

They walked up Rue Blanche together. On the corner of Rue de Douai, they shook hands and parted company, and Maigret headed down Rue Notre-Dame-de-Lorette. When he arrived at his hotel, he was surprised to catch himself whistling.

By ten in the morning, he was ensconced at the Chope du Pont-Neuf, where he had chosen a table that was intermittently in the sun, as the passers-by kept casting shadows. Spring was already in the air. Street life was more cheerful, the sounds sharper.

At Quai des Orfèvres, it was time for the morning briefing. At the end of the long corridor of offices, the head of the Police Judiciaire was meeting his colleagues, who had all brought their case files. Detective Chief Inspector Amadieu was in his element. Maigret could imagine the scenario.

'Well, Amadieu, what's new in the Palestrino case?'

Amadieu leaning forwards, twiddling his moustache, saying with an amiable smile:

'Here are the reports, chief.'

'Is it true that Maigret is in Paris?'

'So rumour has it.'

'So why the hell hasn't he come to see me?'

Maigret smiled. He was certain that this was how the

conversation would go. He could picture Amadieu's long face growing even longer. He could hear him insinuating:

'Perhaps he has his reasons.'

'Do you really think young Philippe fired that shot?'

'I'm not making any accusations, chief. All I know is that his fingerprints are on the gun. We found a second bullet in the wall.'

'Why would he have done that?'

'Panic . . . We're given young inspectors who haven't been trained to—'

Just then, Philippe walked into the Chope du Pont-Neuf and made a beeline for his uncle, who asked:

'What are you drinking?'

'A *café crème*. I've managed to get everything you asked for, but it wasn't easy. Amadieu has got his eye on me! The others are wary of me.'

He wiped the lenses of his glasses and fished some papers out of his pocket.

'First of all, Cageot. I looked him up in the files and copied his details. He was born in Pontoise and he's fifty-nine years old. He started out as a solicitor's clerk in Lyon and he was sentenced to a year for forgery and falsification of records. Three years later, he was given six months for attempted insurance fraud. That was in Marseille.

'There's no trace of him for several years, but then he turned up again in Monte-Carlo, where he worked as a croupier. From that point he was a police informant, which didn't prevent him from being mixed up in a gambling case that was never solved.

'Finally, five years ago, in Paris, he was manager of a

low-down dive called the Cercle de l'Est. The place was soon closed down, but Cageot wasn't bothered. That's the lot! Since then, he's lived in an apartment in Rue des Batignolles where there's just a cleaning woman. He's still a regular visitor to the Ministry of the Interior in Rue des Saussaies and at Quai des Orfèvres. He owns at least three nightclubs which are managed by front men.'

'Pepito?' asked Maigret, who had taken notes.

'Age twenty-nine. Born in Naples. Deported from France twice for drug trafficking. No other offences.'

'Barnabé?'

'Born in Marseille. Age thirty-two. Three convictions, including one for armed robbery.'

'Has the stuff been found at the Floria?'

'Nothing. No drugs, no documents. Pepito's killer took the lot.'

'What's the name of the fellow who bumped into you and then called the police?'

'Joseph Audiat. A former waiter who's mixed up in horse-racing. I think his job is to collect the bets. He is of no fixed address and has his post delivered to the Tabac Fontaine.'

'By the way,' said Maigret, 'I met your lady friend.'

'My lady friend?' echoed Philippe, turning beetroot.

'A tall girl in a green silk dress. You bought her a drink at the Floria. We almost slept together.'

'Well I didn't!' said Philippe. 'If she told you otherwise—'

Lucas had just come in and stood dithering in the doorway. Maigret beckoned him over.

'Are you handling the case?'

'Not exactly, chief. I just wanted to let you know that Cageot is at headquarters again. He arrived a quarter of an hour ago and shut himself up with Detective Chief Inspector Amadieu.'

'Do you want a beer?'

Lucas filled his pipe from Maigret's tobacco pouch. It was the hour when the waiters were setting up, polishing the mirrors with whiting and scattering sawdust between the tables. The owner, already in a black jacket, was inspecting the hors-d'œuvres lined up on a serving table.

'Do you think it's Cageot?' asked Lucas, dropping his voice and reaching for his beer.

'I'm convinced of it.'

'That's no joke!'

Philippe kept quiet, awed by his companions, who had worked together for nearly twenty years. From time to time, between puffs on their pipes, the two veterans would utter a few syllables.

'Did he see you, chief?'

'I went there and told him I'd get him. Waiter! Two more beers!'

'He'll never confess.'

La Samaritaine delivery lorries rumbled past the windows, bright yellow in the sunshine. Long trams followed them, clanging their bells.

'What do you plan to do?'

Maigret shrugged. He had no idea. His beady eyes were staring beyond the bustle of the street at the Palais de Justice on the other side of the Seine. Philippe toyed with his pencil.

'I have to run!' sighed Sergeant Lucas. 'I've got to investigate a kid from Rue Saint-Antoine, some Pole who's been up to some funny business. Will you be here this afternoon?'

'Most likely.'

Maigret rose too. Philippe grew anxious:

'Shall I come with you?'

'I'd rather you didn't. Go back to Quai des Orfèvres. We'll meet back here for lunch.'

Maigret boarded the omnibus and half an hour later he was climbing the stairs to Fernande's apartment. It took her a few minutes to open the door, because she was still in bed. Sunlight was streaming into the room. The sheets on the unmade bed were bright white.

'Already!' exclaimed Fernande, clutching her pyjama top over her chest. 'I was asleep! Wait a moment.'

She went into the kitchen, lit the gas ring and filled a saucepan with water, talking all the while.

'I went to the Tabac Fontaine, like you asked me to. Naturally they aren't wary of me. Did you know that the owner also has a hotel in Avignon?'

'Go on.'

'There was a table where some men were playing cards. Me, I acted like I'd been out all night and was tired.'

'Did you happen to notice a small, dark man called Joseph Audiat?'

'Wait! There was a Joseph, at any rate. He was telling the others how he'd spent the afternoon being questioned by an examining magistrate. But you know how it goes. They play. *Belote! Rebelote!* Your turn, Pierre . . . Then one of them says something . . . Someone answers from the bar . . . Pass! . . . Pass again! . . . Your go, Marcel! . . . The owner was playing too . . . There was an African . . . "Do you want a drink?" a tall, dark-haired man asked me, pointing to a chair near him. "I don't mind if I do." He showed me his hand. "In any case," said the man they called Joseph, "I think it's risky to involve a cop. Tomorrow, they're going to bring me face to face with him. He looks like a right idiot, of course . . ." "Hearts trumps." " *Quatrième haute!*"' Fernande interrupted herself:

'Will you have a cup of coffee too?'

And soon the smell of coffee filled the three-room apartment.

'So anyway, I couldn't suddenly start asking them about Cageot, could I? I said to them, "So do you fellows come here every night?" "Looks like it," said the one sitting next to me. "And you didn't hear anything, last night?"'

Maigret, having removed his coat and hat, had half opened the window, allowing the street noises to enter the room. Fernande went on:

'He gave me a funny look and he said: "Are you a bad girl?" I could see he was getting aroused. Still playing cards, he stroked my knee. And he went on: "Us lot, we don't hear anything, you understand? Apart from Joseph, who saw what he had to see . . ." That made them all roar with laughter. What could I do? I didn't dare move my leg away. "Spades again! *Tierce haute* and *belote!*" "He's one hell of a guy!" said Joseph, who was drinking a hot toddy. But the fellow who was stroking my leg coughed then grumbled:

"I'd rather he didn't spend so much time with the cops, if you know what I mean."'

Maigret felt as if he were in the room. He could have put a name to almost each face. He already knew that the owner ran a brothel in Avignon. And the tall, dark-haired man must be the owner of the Cupidon, in Béziers, and of a brothel in Nîmes. As for the African, he belonged to a local jazz outfit.

'They didn't mention any names?' Maigret asked Fernande, who was stirring her coffee.

'No names. Two or three times they said *the Lawyer*. I thought they meant Cageot. He looks like a degenerate lawyer. But wait, I haven't finished! Aren't you hungry? It must have been three in the morning. You could hear them pulling down the shutters at the Floria. My neighbour, who was still rubbing my knee, was beginning to annoy me. That's when the door opened and Cageot came in. He touched the brim of his hat, but he didn't say a general hello.

'Nobody looked up. You could feel they were all giving him shifty glances. The owner scooted over to the bar.

'"Give me six *Voltigeur* cigars and a box of matches," said Cageot.

'Little Joseph didn't bat an eyelid. He stared at the bottom of his toddy glass. Cageot lit a cigar, put the others in his jacket pocket, and looked for a note in his wallet. You could have heard a pin drop.

'The silence didn't bother him. He turned round, looked at everyone, calmly, coolly, then touched his hat again and left.'

As Fernande dunked her buttered bread in her

coffee, her pyjama top had fallen open, revealing a pert breast.

She must have been in her late twenties, but she had the body of a girl and her barely formed nipples were pale pink.

'They didn't say anything after he left?' questioned Maigret who couldn't help turning down the gas ring on which the kettle was beginning to sing.

'They looked at each other and exchanged winks. The owner sat down again, sighing: "Is that all?" Joseph, who looked awkward, explained: "It's not that he's proud, you know!"'

At this time of day, Rue Blanche was almost provincial. You could hear the clatter of the hooves of the horses harnessed to a heavy brewer's dray.

'The others sniggered,' added Fernande. 'The one who was groping my leg groaned: "It's not that he's proud, no! But he's shrewd enough to land us all in it. I tell you, I'd like it better if he didn't go to Quai des Orfèvres every day!"'

Fernande had told her story taking care not to forget anything.

'Did you go straight home?'

'That wasn't possible.'

Maigret looked none too pleased.

'Oh!' she hastily added, 'I didn't bring him back here. It's best not to show those people that you've got a few bits and pieces. He didn't let me go until five o'clock.'

She rose and went to get a breath of fresh air by the window.

'What should I do now?'

Maigret paced up and down, preoccupied.

'What's his name, your lover-boy?'

'Eugène. There are two gold initials on his cigarette case: E.B.'

'Do you want to go back to the Tabac Fontaine tonight?'

'If I have to.'

'Pay attention to the one called Joseph in particular, the little guy who fetched the police.'

'He took no notice of me.'

'I'm not asking you to do *that*. Just listen carefully to what he says.'

'Now, if you don't mind, I have to clean my place up,' said Fernande tying a kerchief over her hair.

They shook hands. And as he descended the stairs, Maigret had no idea that there would be a raid in Montmartre, and that the police would swoop on the Tabac Fontaine and take Fernande to the station.'

Cageot knew.

'I should inform you of half a dozen women who are in an irregular situation,' he was saying at that very moment to the chief of the vice squad.

Fernande above all, who was going to be carted off in a meat wagon!

4.

Maigret had just finished shaving and was cleaning his razor when there was a knock on his door. It was nine in the morning. He had been awake since eight, but, for once, he had lain in bed for ages watching the sun's slanting rays and listening to the sounds of the city.

'Come in!' he shouted.

And he took a sip of the cold coffee stagnating at the bottom of his cup. Philippe's hesitant footsteps echoed in the room and finally reached the bathroom.

'Good morning, son.'

'Good morning, Uncle.'

Maigret knew from his voice that something was wrong. He buttoned up his shirt and looked at his nephew, who had red eyelids and puffy nostrils like a child who had been crying.

'What's happened?'

'I've been arrested!'

Philippe said this as gloomily as if he were announcing that he would be going in front of a firing squad in five minutes.

He held out a newspaper. Maigret glanced at it while continuing to get dressed.

Despite Inspector Philippe Lauer's denials, examining magistrate Gastambide reportedly decided to have him arrested this morning.

'My photo's splashed all over the front page of the *Excelsior*,' Philippe added melodramatically.

His uncle said nothing. There was nothing to be said. His braces dangling, slippers on his bare feet, he padded to and fro in the sunshine, hunting for his pipe, then his tobacco and finally a box of matches.

'You didn't drop by there this morning?' asked Maigret.

'I've come from Rue des Dames. I saw the paper when I was having my coffee and croissant in Boulevard des Batignolles.'

It was an exceptional morning. The air was fresh, the sun joyful, and the intense, animated bustle of Paris a frenzied dance. Maigret opened the window and the room reverberated with the throbbing life of the riverbanks, while the slow-moving Seine shimmered in the sunlight.

'Well, you have to go, my boy! What can I say?'

He didn't want to get all sentimental over this kid who had forsaken his green valley in the Vosges for the corridors of the Police Judiciaire!

'Naturally, it won't be as cushy as home!'

His mother was Madame Maigret's sister, and that said it all. She mollycoddled the boy: *Philippe will be home soon . . . Philippe will be hungry . . . Have Philippe's shirts been ironed? . . .*

And tasty little dishes, home-made desserts and liqueurs! And sprigs of lavender in the linen cupboard!

'There's something else,' said Philippe while his uncle adjusted his detachable collar. 'Last night I went to the Floria.'

'Of course!'

'Why of course?'

'Because I advised you not to go there. Now what have you done?'

'Nothing. I chatted with that girl, Fernande, you know. She hinted that she was working with you and that she had some mission to carry out at the café on the corner of Rue de Douai. Since I was leaving anyway, I followed her, instinctively. It was on my way home. But on her way out of the café, she was yelled at by inspectors from the vice squad and bundled into a meat wagon.'

'You tried to step in, I'll bet!'

Philippe looked shamefaced.

'What did they say?'

'That they knew what they were doing.'

'Off you go now,' sighed Maigret, hunting for his tie. 'Don't worry.'

He put his hands on Philippe's shoulders, kissed him on both cheeks and, to cut the scene short, suddenly pretended to be very busy. Only when the door had opened and closed behind Philippe again did he look up, hunch his shoulders and mutter a few garbled syllables.

The first thing he did once on the riverbank was to buy the *Excelsior* from a news kiosk and look at the photo which was indeed on the front page with the caption:

Inspector Philippe Lauer, accused of killing Pepito Palestrino, who was under surveillance.

Maigret walked slowly over the Pont-Neuf. The previous evening, he had not gone inside the Floria but had paid a visit to Rue des Batignolles to sniff around Cageot's place. He lived in a residential building dating from the 1880s, like most of the apartment blocks in the neighbourhood. The corridor and the staircase were poorly lit. It was easy to imagine the dark, dismal apartments, grubby curtains at the windows and furniture with faded velvet upholstery.

Cageot's apartment was on the mezzanine. There was no one around at this time of day and Maigret had entered the building as if he were a regular visitor. He wandered up to the fourth floor and then came back down again.

There was a safety lock on Cageot's door, otherwise Maigret might have given in to temptation. He walked past the lodge and the concierge, face pressed up against the window, stared after him for a while.

What could that matter? Maigret crossed almost the entire city on foot, his hands in his pockets, the same thoughts going round and round in his head.

Somewhere – at the Tabac Fontaine or elsewhere – there was a small group of crooks who were happily going about their illicit business. Pepito had been one of them. Barnabé too.

And one by one, Cageot, the big boss, was eliminating them, or having them eliminated.

Gangland killings! The police would hardly have bothered about them if that idiot Philippe—

Maigret had arrived at Quai des Orfèvres. Two inspectors on their way out greeted him with unconcealed surprise, and he went through the entrance, crossed the courtyard and walked past the vice squad.

Upstairs it was time for the morning briefing. In the vast

corridor, fifty police officers stood in huddles, speaking in loud voices and passing on intelligence and records. Sometimes an office door opened and a name was yelled and summoned inside.

Maigret's arrival caused a few moments' silence and unease. But he sauntered past the groups looking perfectly at home, and the officers resumed their confabs to keep up appearances.

To the right was the chief's waiting room furnished with red velvet armchairs. Sitting in a corner, a lone visitor was waiting. Chin cupped in his hands, Philippe stared fixedly ahead of him.

Maigret walked off in the opposite direction, reached the end of the corridor and knocked at the last door.

'Come in!' answered a voice from inside.

And everyone saw him enter Detective Chief Inspector Amadieu's office, hat in hand.

'Hello, Maigret.'

'Hello, Amadieu.'

They touched fingertips as they used to do when they saw each other every morning. Amadieu signalled to an inspector to leave, then murmured:

'Did you want to talk to me?'

Maigret perched on the edge of the desk in a familiar pose and picked up a box of matches from the table to light his pipe.

His colleague had pushed back his chair and tilted it backwards.

'How's country life?'

'Fine, thanks. How are things here?'

'Still the same. I have to see the chief in five minutes.'

Maigret pretended not to know what that meant and began unbuttoning his overcoat, slowly and deliberately. He was very much at home in this office, which had been his for ten years.

'Are you worried about your nephew?' blurted out Amadieu, who was unable to keep quiet any longer. 'I want you to know that I'm even more concerned than you are. I'm the one who's carrying the can. It's gone all the way to the top, you know. The minister himself sent a note to the chief. I'm not even involved any more. It's the examining magistrate who's in charge. Gastambide was there in your day, wasn't he?'

The telephone rang. Amadieu held the receiver to his ear and muttered:

'. . . Yes, chief . . . Very good, chief . . . In a few minutes . . . I'm not alone . . . Yes . . . That's correct . . .'

Maigret knew what this conversation was about. At the other end of the corridor, Philippe had just been called into the chief's office.

'Did you want to ask me something?' said Amadieu, getting to his feet. 'You heard. The chief wants me.'

'Just a couple of questions. First of all, was Cageot aware that Pepito was about to be arrested?'

'I don't know. Besides, I don't see how that's relevant.'

'I'm sorry. I know Cageot. I know he's an informer. I also know that sometimes there's careless talk in front of informers. Did he come here two or three days before the murder?'

'I think so. Yes, I recall—'

'Another question: Do you know the address of Joseph Audiat, that waiter who was walking down Rue Fontaine and just happened to bump into Philippe?'

'He sleeps at a hotel in Rue Lepic, if I'm not mistaken.'

'Have you checked out Cageot's alibi?'

Amadieu feigned a smile.

'Now look, Maigret, I know how to do my job!'

But there was more to come. On the desk, Maigret had spotted a yellow cardboard folder with the vice squad's letterhead.

'Is that the report on Fernande Bosquet's arrest already?'

Amadieu looked away. He had seemed about to give Maigret a clear explanation, but now his hand was on the door knob and he merely mumbled:

'What do you mean?'

'I mean that Cageot had a girl arrested by the Vice. Where is she now?'

'I don't know.'

'May I have a quick look at the file?'

It was hard to say no. Maigret leaned over, read a few lines and concluded:

'She's probably having her fingerprints done as we speak.'

The telephone rang again. Amadieu raised his hand.

'I'm sorry, but—'

'I know. Mustn't keep the chief waiting.'

Maigret buttoned up his overcoat and left the office at the same time as Amadieu. Instead of heading back down the stairs, he walked with him to the waiting room with red velvet armchairs.

'Would you ask the chief if he can see me?'

Amadieu pushed open a padded door. The office boy also vanished inside the head of the Police Judiciaire's office where Philippe was being grilled. Maigret stood waiting, hat in hand.

'The chief is very busy and requests that you come back this afternoon.'

Maigret turned and walked back through the knots of inspectors. His expression was a little grim, but he wanted to keep up appearances. He gave a joyless smile.

He did not go back out into the street, but sneaked off down the narrow corridors and up the winding staircases that led to the top floor of the Palais de Justice. He found his way to the criminal records department and pushed open the door. The women's session was over. In the grey room around fifty men who had been arrested the previous night were getting undressed, leaving their clothes in little piles on the benches lining the walls.

Once naked, one by one they went into the next room where staff in black overalls took their fingerprints, sat them down on the anthropometric chair and shouted out their measurements like sales assistants in a department store announcing a sale at the till.

There was a smell of sweat and filth. Most of the men were bewildered, awkward in their nakedness, allowing themselves to be shoved around from pillar to post and trying to obey instructions, many of them confused because they did not speak French.

Maigret cordially shook hands with the staff and heard the inevitable platitudes:

'Popping in to say hello?' 'How's life in the country?' 'It must be gorgeous in this weather!'

The neon lamp shed a crude light in the little room where the photographer worked.

'Were there a lot of women, this morning?'

'Seven.'

'Have you got their records?'

They were lying on a table since they had not yet been filed. The third one was Fernande's, with the prints of her five fingers, a clumsy signature and a horribly realistic mug shot.

'Did she say anything? Did she cry?'

'No. She was very docile.'

'Do you know where she's been taken?'

'I don't know whether they let her go or whether they'll make her do a few days in Saint-Lazare.'

Maigret's gaze roved over the naked men who stood in rows like soldiers. He raised his hand to his hat and said:

'Goodbye!'

'Are you leaving so soon?'

He was already on the stairs, where there was not a single step that he hadn't trodden a thousand times. Another staircase, to the left, narrower than the first, led to the laboratory whose every nook and cranny, every vial, he knew.

He was back on the second floor just after the troop of inspectors had left. Visitors began to take their places outside various doors – people who had been summoned, or who had come to lodge a complaint, or who had something they wanted to report.

Maigret had spent most of his life in this atmosphere but now he looked around him with a sort of disgust.

Was Philippe still in the chief's office? Probably not! By now he would have been arrested and two of his colleagues would be escorting him to the examining magistrate's chambers!

What had been said to him, behind the padded door? Had they spoken to him honestly and plainly?

'You have committed a blunder. The evidence against you is such that the public would not understand if you remained at liberty. But we will endeavour to uncover the truth. You will remain one of us.'

That was probably not what had been said. Maigret thought he could hear the chief, uncomfortable while waiting for Amadieu, mutter between coughs:

'Inspector, I am extremely displeased with you. It was easier for you to get into the police than for anyone else thanks to your uncle. Have you shown yourself worthy of that favour?'

And Amadieu would go further:

'As of now, you are in the hands of the examining magistrate. With the best will in the world, there is nothing we can do for you.'

And yet this Amadieu, with his long pale face and his brown moustache, which he was always tapering, was not a bad man. He had a wife and three children, including a daughter he wanted to provide with a dowry. He had always believed that everyone around him was scheming, that they all wanted his job and were constantly seeking to compromise him.

As for the chief, in two years' time he would reach retirement age and until then it was best to avoid trouble.

This was a standard gangland killing, in other words, a run-of-the-mill case. Were they going to risk complications by protecting a rookie inspector who had gone astray and was Maigret's nephew to boot?

Cageot was a crook and everyone knew it. He himself didn't even hide it. He cashed in on all sides. And when he sold someone to the police, it was because that person was no longer useful to him.

Nevertheless, Cageot was a dangerous criminal. He had friends, connections. And above all, he was good at protecting himself. They would get him one day, for sure. They had him in their sights. They had checked his alibi and the investigation would follow the proper course.

But there was no need for overzealousness! And there was certainly no need for Maigret, with his habit of putting his foot in it.

Maigret had reached the little paved courtyard where a morose crowd waited outside the juvenile court. Despite the sunshine, there was a chill in the air and in the shade there was still a dusting of frost between the flagstones.

'That idiot Philippe!' grumbled Maigret almost sick with revulsion.

For he was well aware that he was going round and round like a circus horse. There was no point waiting for a brainwave; in police matters, brainwaves were of no use. Nor was it a matter of discovering a phenomenal lead, or a clue that had eluded everyone else.

It was simpler and more brutal. Cageot had killed Pepito, or had him killed. The challenge was to get Cageot finally to admit that this was the truth.

Now Maigret was strolling along the riverbank, close to the laundry boat. He did not have the power to summon Cageot to an office and lock him in for a few hours, or to repeat the same question a hundred times, roughing him up if necessary to make him crack.

Nor could he summon the café owner, the waiter or the men who played *belote* every night a hundred metres from the Floria.

He had barely started using Fernande when she had literally been snatched away from him.

He reached the Chope du Pont-Neuf, pushed open the glazed door and went over to shake hands with Lucas, who was sitting at the bar.

'How are things, chief?'

'Not good!' replied Maigret.

'It's tough, isn't it?'

It wasn't tough. It was a hopelessly tragic situation.

'I'm getting old! Maybe it's the effect of rural life.'

'What are you drinking?'

'I'll have a Pernod!'

He said that almost defiantly. He remembered that he had promised to write to his wife, but he hadn't felt up to it.

'Is there some way I can help?'

Lucas was a curious character, always badly dressed, puny into the bargain, who had neither wife nor family. Maigret let his gaze rove around the place, which was beginning to fill up, and he had to crease his eyes when he turned to the window where the sun was streaming in.

'Have you worked with Philippe?'

'A couple of times.'

'Was he very disagreeable?'

'There are people who resent him because he doesn't say much. He's shy, you know. Have they banged him up?'

'Cheers.'

Lucas was concerned to see Maigret so tight-lipped.

'What are you going to do, chief?'

'I know I can trust you, so I'll tell you. I'm going to do *everything* that's necessary. Do you understand? It's best that someone knows, so if anything were to happen—'

He wiped his mouth on the back of his hand, and tapped a coin on the bar to attract the waiter's attention.

'Leave it! It's my round,' said Lucas.

'If you insist. I'll buy a round when this is over. Good-bye, Lucas.'

'Goodbye, chief.'

Lucas' hand lingered for a moment in Maigret's rough paw.

'All the same, you will take care, won't you?'

And Maigret, on his feet, boomed:

'I cannot stand cretins!'

He walked off alone. He had plenty of time, since he had no idea where he was going.

5.

As Maigret pushed open the door of the Tabac Fontaine, at around 1.30, the owner, who had just risen, was slowly making his way down a spiral staircase into the back of the café. Although not as tall as Maigret, he was just as broad and burly. As he crossed the room, he exuded a whiff of the bathroom – his hair reeked of cologne and there were traces of talcum powder behind his ears. He wore neither a jacket nor a collar. His lightly starched shirt was snowy white, fastened by a swivel stud.

He went behind the bar, shoving the waiter roughly aside, grabbed a bottle of white wine and a glass, diluted the wine with mineral water, threw back his head and gargled.

At that hour, there were just a few passing customers snatching a hurried coffee. Maigret went and sat by the window, but the owner, oblivious of him, tied on a blue apron and turned to a blonde girl seated at the till of the cigarette counter.

He said no more to her than to the waiter, opened the cash register, looked at a notebook and stretched, now fully awake. His day was beginning, and the first thing he noticed on inspecting his realm was Maigret staring placidly at him.

They had never met, but the owner still knitted his thick,

black eyebrows. He appeared to be racking his brains. Unable to place Maigret, he scowled. And yet he could never have foreseen that this placid customer was going to sit there for twelve full hours!

Maigret's first task was to go over to the till and say to the girl:

'Have you got a telephone token?'

The booth was in a corner of the café. It only had a frosted glass door, and Maigret, sensing the owner had his eye on him, jiggled the handset making a series of loud clicks. Meanwhile, using the pen-knife he was holding in his other hand, he cut the cable at the point where it went under the floor, so that no one would notice that it had been severed.

'Hello! . . . Hello! . . .' he yelled.

He emerged fuming.

'Is your telephone out of order?'

The owner glanced over at the cashier, who looked surprised.

'It was working a few minutes ago. Lucien telephoned for some croissants. Didn't you, Lucien?'

'Barely a quarter of an hour ago,' confirmed the waiter.

The owner wasn't suspicious yet, but he was still watching Maigret covertly. He went into the booth and tried to make a call, persisting for a good ten minutes without noticing the severed cable.

Impassive, Maigret had returned to his table and ordered a beer. He was stocking up on patience. He knew that he was going to have to sit on that same chair for hours, in front of that fake mahogany pedestal table, confronted with the sight of the pewter bar and the glazed booth where the girl sold tobacco and cigarettes.

As he came out of the telephone booth, the owner kicked the door shut, walked over to the doorway and sniffed the air of the street for a moment. He stood very close to Maigret, who was staring fixedly at him. Finally becoming aware of that penetrating gaze, he spun round.

Maigret didn't move a muscle. He was still wearing his overcoat and hat, as if about to leave.

'Lucien! Run next door and telephone for someone to come and repair the phone.'

The waiter hurried out, a dirty napkin over his arm, and the owner himself served two builders who came in, their faces clown-like under an almost even layer of plaster dust.

An atmosphere of doubt hung in the air for perhaps another ten minutes. When Lucien announced that the engineer would not be coming until the next day, the owner turned to Maigret again and muttered under his breath:

'Bastard!'

He could have meant the tardy engineer, but the insult was chiefly addressed to the customer in whom he finally recognized a policeman.

It was 2.30 and this was the prologue to a long, drawn-out performance, which eluded everybody present. The owner's name was Louis. Customers who knew him came and shook his hand, exchanged a few words with him. Louis himself rarely served. Most of the time, he stayed in the background, behind the bar, between the waiter and the girl on the cigarette counter.

And he watched Maigret over their heads. He made no

bones about it, and Maigret watched him with equal brazenness. The situation could have been comical, for they were both big, broad and heavy, and they were trying to outstare each other.

Neither was a fool, either. Louis knew exactly what he was doing when, from time to time, he glanced at the glass door, afraid of seeing a certain person walk in.

At that hour, Rue Fontaine was bustling with everyday activities like any other Paris street. Opposite the bar there was an Italian grocery where the local housewives came to do their shopping.

'Waiter! A calvados.'

The lethargic blonde cashier stared at Maigret with mounting curiosity. Meanwhile, the waiter had intuited that something was amiss, although he didn't know what exactly, and he gave the owner an occasional wink.

It was just after three when a big, light-coloured limousine pulled up outside. A tall, youngish, dark-haired man with a scar on his left cheek alighted and entered the café, extending his hand over the bar.

'Hello, Louis.'

'Hello, Eugène.'

Maigret had a direct view of Louis, and he could see the newcomer's reflection in the mirror.

'A mint-soda, Lucien. And make it quick.'

He was one of the *belote* players, probably the owner of a brothel in Béziers that Fernande had mentioned. He wore a silk shirt and his clothes were well tailored. He too smelled fragrant.

'Have you seen the—'

He broke off mid-sentence. Louis had signalled to him that someone was eavesdropping and Eugène looked up at Maigret's reflection.

'Hmm! Where's that iced soda, Lucien?'

He took a cigarette from a monogrammed case, and lit it from his lighter.

'Nice weather, isn't it!' said the owner, with irony, still eyeing Maigret.

'Nice weather indeed. But there's a funny smell in here.'

'What smell?'

'Something fishy.'

They both roared with laughter, while Maigret puffed gently on his pipe.

'See you later?' queried Eugène, extending his hand once again.

He wanted to know if they'd be meeting up as usual.

'See you later.'

This conversation galvanized Louis, who grabbed a dirty cloth and, with a grin, came over to Maigret.

'May I?'

He wiped the table so clumsily that he knocked over the glass, spilling the contents on to Maigret's trousers.

'Lucien! Bring the gentleman another glass.'

And, by way of apology:

'No extra charge!'

Maigret gave a vague smile in return.

By five o'clock the street lamps were lit, but it was still light enough outside to identify the customers as they crossed the road and reached for the door handle.

When Joseph Audiat walked in, Louis and Maigret looked at each other, as of one accord, and from that moment it was almost as if they had been exchanging protracted secrets. There was no need to mention the Floria, or Pepito, or Cageot.

Maigret knew, and Louis knew that he knew.

'Evening, Louis!'

Audiat was a short man, dressed in black from head to foot, with a slightly crooked nose and eyes that darted everywhere. He walked up to the bar and held his hand out to the blonde cashier, saying:

'Hello, sweetheart.'

Then to Lucien:

'A Pernod, young man.'

He talked a lot. He gave the impression of an actor on stage. But Maigret soon discerned a certain anxiety beneath his façade. Audiat also had a nervous twitch. As soon as his smile left his lips, he automatically struggled to recompose it.

'No one here yet?'

The café was empty. There were only two customers standing at the bar.

'Eugène's been in.'

The owner re-enacted the scene he had played earlier, pointing out Maigret to Audiat who, less diplomatic than Eugène, swung round, looked Maigret in the eye and spat on the floor.

'Anything else?' he said.

'Nothing. Did you win?'

'No. Zilch! I was given a tip that backfired. I was in with

a chance for the third race, but the horse missed the start. Give me a packet of Gauloises, sweetheart.'

He could not keep still; he kept shifting from one foot to the other, gesticulating and waggling his head.

'Can I make a phone call?'

Louis looked daggers at Maigret.

'No you can't. The gentleman over there wrecked the phone.'

It was open war. Audiat was ill at ease. He was afraid of making a blunder, for he had no idea what had happened before his arrival.

'Are we seeing each other this evening?'

'As usual!'

Audiat downed his Pernod and left. Meanwhile, Louis came and sat down at the table next to Maigret, where the waiter brought him a hot meal which he had cooked on the gas ring in the back.

'Waiter!' Maigret called out.

'Here! Nine francs seventy-five—'

'Bring me two ham sandwiches and a beer.'

Louis was eating some reheated sauerkraut with two appetizing-looking sausages.

'Is there any ham left, Monsieur Louis?'

'There must be an old piece in the icebox.'

He chewed noisily, crudely exaggerating his movements. The waiter brought Maigret two dry, shrivelled sandwiches, but he pretended not to notice.

'Waiter! Some mustard—'

'There isn't any.'

The two hours that followed went faster, for the bar was

invaded by passers-by dropping in for an aperitif. The owner condescended to serve them himself. The door kept opening and closing, sending a blast of cold air in Maigret's direction each time.

Now the temperature had dropped to freezing. For a while, the passing omnibuses were crammed full, and there were passengers standing on the platform at the rear. Then, gradually, the street grew empty. The seven o'clock flurry gave way to an unexpected quiet, a prelude to the very different bustle of the evening.

The toughest hour was between eight and nine. The place was deserted. The blonde girl behind the till had been replaced by a woman in her forties, who began sorting all the coins from the cash register into piles. Louis had gone up to his room, and when he came back down, he was wearing a jacket and tie.

Joseph Audiat was the first to put in an appearance, a few minutes after nine. He looked around for Maigret and strolled over to Louis.

'Everything OK?'

'Everything OK. There's no reason why it wouldn't be, is there?'

But Louis did not have the same energy as earlier. He was tired, and did not look at Maigret with the same cockiness. And Maigret himself seemed to exhibit a certain weariness. He must have drunk a little of everything – beer, coffee, calvados, mineral water. Seven or eight saucers were piled up on the table in front of him, and he had to order another drink.

'Look! Here come Eugène and his friend.'

The pale-blue limousine had drawn up alongside the kerb again, and two men came into the bar, Eugène first of all, dressed as he had been that afternoon, then a younger, timid-looking man who smiled at everyone.

'What about Oscar?'

'He's bound to come.'

Eugène winked, jerking his head in Maigret's direction, moved two tables together and went over to fetch the red mat and the chips from a drawer.

'Shall we begin?'

They were all putting on an act. But it was Eugène and the owner who were calling the tune. Especially Eugène, who was freshly arrived on the scene. He had brilliant white teeth and a genuine cheerfulness, and women must have gone crazy over him.

'At least we'll be able to see clearly tonight!' he said.

'Why?' asked Audiat, who was always a bit slow on the uptake.

'Because we have a luminary among us!'

That luminary was Maigret, who was smoking his pipe less than a metre away from the players.

Louis picked up the slate and the chalk with a ritual gesture. He was the one who usually kept score. He drew the columns headed with the players' initials.

'What are you drinking?' asked the waiter.

Eugène narrowed his eyes, glanced over at Maigret's calvados and replied:

'The same as the gentleman over there!'

'A strawberry cordial,' said Audiat, on edge.

The fourth man had a strong Marseille accent and could

not have been in Paris long. He took his cue from Eugène, for whom he appeared to have a profound admiration.

'The hunting season's not over yet, is it, Louis?'

This time it was Louis who was bemused.

'How do I know? Why are you asking?'

'Because I was thinking about going after rabbits.'

Again, it was Maigret who was the butt of his comment. The explanation followed, as the cards were dealt and each player arranged them in a fan in his left hand.

'I went to see the man, earlier.'

Which translated as: 'I went to warn Cageot'.

Audiat abruptly looked up.

'What did he say?'

Louis frowned, probably thinking that they were going too far.

'He's laughing! Apparently he's on home ground and he's planning a little party.'

'Diamonds trumps . . . *Tierce haute* . . . OK?'

'Four of a kind.'

Eugène was all keyed up and it was clear he was not concentrating on the game but on coming up with fresh witticisms.

'The Parisians,' he stated, 'go and spend their holidays in the country – in the Loire, for example. The funny thing is, that the people from the Loire come and spend their holidays in Paris.'

At last! He hadn't been able to resist the urge to let Maigret know that he knew all about him. And Maigret sat there, puffing away on his pipe and warming his calvados in the hollow of his hand before taking a sip.

'Keep your eyes on the game,' retorted Louis, who kept darting anxious glances in the direction of the door.

'Trumps . . . and double trumps. A twenty-point bonus, plus ten for the last trick . . .'

An individual who looked like a modest Montmartre shopkeeper walked in and went over to wedge himself between Eugène and his friend from Marseille, without saying a word. He shook both their hands and sat slightly back, still without opening his mouth.

'All right?' asked Louis.

The newcomer's lips parted, and a thin, reedy sound came out. He had lost his voice.

'All right!'

'You got it?' Eugène bawled in his ear, revealing that the man was deaf as well.

'Twigged what?' replied the reedy voice.

They must have kicked him under the table. Finally the deaf man's gaze lighted on Maigret and rested on him for a long moment. He gave a faint smile.

'I get it.'

'Clubs trumps . . . Pass . . .'

'Pass . . .'

Rue Fontaine was coming back to life. The neon signs were lit and the doormen were at their posts on the pavement. The Floria's doorman came in to buy cigarettes, but no one took any notice of him.

'Hearts trumps . . .'

Maigret was hot. He felt stiff all over but he gave no sign of it and his expression remained the same as when he had begun his long vigil.

'I say!' said Eugène suddenly to his hard-of-hearing neighbour, whom Maigret had recognized as the owner of a brothel in Rue de Provence. 'What do you call a locksmith who doesn't make locks any more?'

The comical aspect of this conversation came from the fact that Eugène had to shout, while the other man answered in an angelic voice:

'A locksmith who—? I don't know.'

'Well, I'd call him a nobody.'

He played a card, picked up and played again.

'And a cop who's no longer a cop?'

The penny had dropped. His neighbour's face lit up and his voice was reedier than ever as he said:

'A nobody!'

Then they all burst out laughing, even Audiat, who gave a snigger. Something was stopping him from joining wholeheartedly in the general mirth. He was visibly anxious, despite the presence of his friends. And it was not solely on account of Maigret.

'Léon!' he shouted to the night waiter. 'Bring me a brandy and water.'

'You're drinking brandy now?'

Eugène had noticed that Audiat was losing his nerve and he was keeping a close eye on him.

'You'd better go easy.'

'Go easy on what?'

'How many Pernods did you have before dinner?'

'Damn you!' replied Audiat stubbornly.

'Calm down, boys,' broke in Louis. 'Spades trumps!'

By midnight, their cheerfulness was more forced. Maigret

was still sitting immobile in his overcoat, his pipe in his mouth. He looked like part of the furniture. Or even better, he blended in with the walls. Only his eyes were alive, roving slowly from one player to the other.

Audiat had been the first to display signs of unease, and then the deaf man soon began to show some impatience. At length, he stood up:

'I have to go to a funeral tomorrow. I should go to bed.'

'Oh, drop dead!' said Eugène under his breath, certain he wouldn't be heard.

He said that the way he would have said anything else, to keep his spirits up.

'Rebelote . . . and trumps . . . and trumps again . . . Give me your cards . . .'

Despite the disapproving looks he was getting, Audiat had drunk three brandies and his face was furrowed. He had turned pale and his forehead was clammy.

'Where are you going?'

'I'm off too,' he said, rising.

He clearly felt sick. He had drunk his third brandy to perk himself up, but it had finished him off. Louis and Eugène exchanged glances.

'You look like a wet rag,' Eugène said after a moment.

It was just after one o'clock in the morning. Maigret took out his money and put it on the table. Eugène drew Audiat into a corner and spoke to him in hushed but urgent tones. Audiat was reluctant, but eventually allowed himself to be persuaded.

'See you tomorrow!' he said, his hand on the door handle.

'Waiter! How much?'

The saucers rattled. Maigret buttoned up his overcoat, filled a fresh pipe and lit it with the gas lighter by the bar.

'Good night, gentlemen.'

He left the café and identified the sound of Audiat's retreating footsteps. Meanwhile, Eugène slipped behind the bar, as if to have a word with the owner. Louis immediately understood and discreetly opened a drawer. Eugène plunged his hand inside then put it in his pocket and headed for the door with the man from Marseille in tow.

'See you later,' he said, stepping out into the night.

6.

In the glow from the nightclubs' neon signs, Rue Fontaine was busy with doormen on the pavement and drivers manoeuvring to park their cars. It was only after Place Blanche, when Maigret and his quarry turned right on to Boulevard Rochechouart, that the situation became clearer.

Joseph Audiat walked ahead with a feverish, irregular step, never once turning round.

Twenty metres behind him came Maigret's burly form taking great, calm strides, his hands thrust in his pockets.

Audiat and Maigret's footsteps echoed each other in the silence of the night, Audiat's more rapid, Maigret's tread heavier and more solemn.

Behind them, the purring of Eugène's engine could be heard – for Eugène and the man from Marseille had jumped into the car. They drove at a crawl, hugging the kerb and trying to keep a distance from the two men. Sometimes they had to change gear to maintain their speed. Sometimes too they would put on a sudden spurt and then slow down to allow Audiat and Maigret to get ahead.

Maigret had no need to look over his shoulder. He knew what was going on. He was aware that the big blue limousine was behind him. He could picture the faces behind the windscreen.

It was classic. He was following Audiat because he had the feeling that Audiat would allow himself to be intimidated more easily than the others. Meanwhile, the others, who knew this, were following him in turn.

At first, this made Maigret smile inwardly.

Then, he was no longer smiling, but frowning. Audiat was not heading towards Rue Lepic, where he had a room, nor towards the centre of Paris. He continued along the boulevard beneath the overground section of the métro in the direction of La Chapelle, without stopping at the Barbès intersection.

It was highly unlikely that he had any business in this neighbourhood at such an hour. There could only be one explanation. Audiat had been instructed by the two men in the car to lure Maigret into the deserted back streets.

Already, the only signs of life were the occasional girl hidden in the shadows, or the hesitant form of a North African going from one to the other before making up his mind.

Maigret did not feel frightened straight away. He remained calm, puffing away on his pipe and listening to his footsteps, as regular as a pendulum.

The boulevard passed over the railway lines coming out of the Gare du Nord, which loomed in the distance with its illuminated clock and empty platforms. The time was 2.30. The car was still purring behind them, when, for no reason, it gave a little hoot of its horn. Then Audiat began walking faster, so fast that he seemed to be trying not to run.

For no apparent reason either, he crossed the road. Maigret

crossed too. For a second, he was sideways on. He saw the car out of the corner of his eye, and that was when it dawned on him what they were up to.

The overground métro made the boulevard darker than any other part of Paris. A police cycle patrol rode past and one of the officers turned round to look at the car, saw nothing untoward and vanished with his colleagues.

The pace was hotting up. After a hundred metres, Audiat crossed the road again, but this time he lost his cool and ran the last few steps. Maigret stopped and he could hear the car revving up. The situation was perfectly clear. There were beads of perspiration on his forehead, for it was pure chance that he had avoided being run over.

So that was it! Audiat's job was to entice him through the empty streets. And then, when Maigret was halfway across the road, the car would mow him down.

As if in a nightmare, Maigret was conscious of the sleek limousine gliding through the streets and its two occupants, especially Eugène, with his brilliant white teeth and angelic smile, sitting with his hands on the wheel waiting for the right moment.

Could this be called a crime? Maigret was in danger of dying a stupid and horrible death any moment now: lying in the dirt, severely wounded, and howling with pain for hours before anyone would come to his aid.

It was too late to turn back. In any case, he didn't want to. He was no longer counting on Audiat, he had abandoned his plan of catching up with him and getting him to talk, but he was determined to continue following him. It was a question of self-respect.

His only precaution was to take his gun out of his trouser pocket and to cock it.

Then he walked a little faster. Instead of staying twenty metres behind Audiat, he was so close on his heels that Audiat thought Maigret was going to arrest him, and he too hastened his step. For a few seconds, it was comical, and the two men in the car must have realized what was going on because they came much closer.

The trees on the boulevard and the pillars supporting the overhead métro filed past. Audiat was afraid, afraid of Maigret and perhaps too of his accomplices. When the car hooted once more to prompt him to cross the road, he stopped, breathless, on the kerb.

Close on his heels, Maigret saw the car's headlamps, Audiat's soft hat and anxious eyes.

He was about to step off the pavement close behind his companion when a sixth sense held him back. Perhaps Audiat had the same intuition, but for him it was too late. He was already in the road, advancing one metre, two metres . . .

Maigret opened his mouth to shout a warning. He could see that the two men in the car, tired of this fruitless chase, had suddenly decided to put their foot down, even if it meant hitting their comrade at the same time as Maigret.

There was no scream. A rush of air, the sound of an engine going at full throttle. A dull thud too, and perhaps a vague shout.

The car's red rear lights were already receding, and then it vanished down a side street. On the ground, the little man in black was struggling to raise himself up on his hands, gazing wild-eyed at Maigret.

He looked like a madman or a child. His face was covered in dust and blood. His nose had changed shape, which distorted his entire face.

He managed to sit up and raise a hand to his forehead, limply, as in a dream, grimacing.

Maigret gathered him up and sat him down on the kerb, and, without thinking, went to pick up the hat that was sitting in the middle of the road. Then it took him a few moments to recover his own equilibrium, even though he had not been hit.

There were no passers-by. A taxi could be heard, but it was a long way off, probably near Barbès.

'You had a narrow escape!' grunted Maigret, leaning over the injured man.

He probed Audiat's head with his thumbs, slowly, to check whether his skull was fractured. He flexed his legs one after the other, for his trousers were torn, or rather ripped off below the right knee, and Maigret glimpsed an ugly wound.

Audiat seemed to have lost not only the power of speech, but also his mind. His jaw worked up and down, as if to get rid of a nasty taste in his mouth.

Maigret looked up. He had heard the sound of an engine. He was convinced it was Eugène's car driving down a back street. Then the noise drew closer and the blue limousine shot across the boulevard barely a hundred metres from the two men.

They could not stay there. Eugène and his sidekick would not go away. They wanted to know what was going to happen. They drove around the neighbourhood in another big circle, the purring of the engine barely audible in the still night. This time, they drove along the boulevard within a few metres of Audiat. Maigret held his breath, expecting gunfire.

'They'll be back,' he thought. 'And next time . . .'

He lifted Audiat, carried him across the road and sat him down on the ground behind a tree.

And the car did drive past again. Eugène failed to spot the two men and pulled up a hundred metres further on. There must have been a brief discussion between him and the other man, and the outcome was that they gave up the chase.

Audiat groaned and writhed as the light from a gas lamp revealed a huge pool of blood on the ground in the spot where he had been knocked over.

There was nothing they could do but wait. Maigret did not dare leave the injured man to go off in search of a taxi, and he was loath to ring a doorbell and have a crowd gather. They only had to wait for ten minutes before a half-drunk Algerian came past, and Maigret got him to understand that he must fetch a taxi.

The night was cold. The sky had the same icy tinge as the night Maigret had left Meung. From time to time the whistle of a freight train reached them from the Gare du Nord.

'It hurts!' said Audiat at last in a mournful tone.

And he looked up at Maigret as if expecting him to alleviate his suffering.

Fortunately, the Algerian had done as he had been asked and a taxi pulled up. The driver was wary:

'Are you sure it was an accident?'

He couldn't make up his mind whether to turn off the engine and help Maigret or not.

'If you don't believe me, take us to the police station,' Maigret replied.

The driver was won over and a quarter of an hour later they pulled up opposite the Hôtel des Quais, where Maigret was staying.

Audiat, who had not closed his eyes, was watching people and things with such an ineffable gentleness that the sight made people smile. The hotel doorman misinterpreted it.

'Your friend looks as though he's had one too many.'

'Perhaps he was a bit drunk. A car knocked him over.'

They carried Audiat up to the room. Maigret ordered a rum and had towels brought. He did not need any help for the rest. While people slept in the neighbouring room, he silently removed his shoes, his jacket and his detachable collar and rolled up his shirt sleeves.

Half an hour later, he was still working on Audiat, who was stretched out on the bed, scrawny and naked, with the mark of his garters on his calves. The ugliest wound was the one on his knee. Maigret disinfected and dressed it. He had put sticking plasters on the few minor scratches and finally got the injured man to drink a large glass of rum.

The radiator was scalding hot. The curtains weren't drawn, and the moon was visible against a patch of sky.

'Well, your friends are utter bastards, aren't they?' sighed Maigret suddenly.

Audiat pointed to his jacket and asked for a cigarette.

'What alerted me was that you were so twitchy. You'd guessed that they'd go after you too!'

His gaze steadier, Audiat eyed Maigret with suspicion. When he did open his mouth, it was to ask a question.

'What does it matter to you?'

'Keep still, you're still very shaken. Let me tell you why it matters to me. A thug – someone you know – killed Pepito, probably because he was afraid he'd say too much about the Barnabé business. At around two in the morning, the thug in question came looking for you at the Tabac Fontaine.'

Audiat knitted his brow and stared at the wall.

'You remember! Cageot called you outside. He asked you to bump into the fellow who'd be coming out of the Floria at any moment. And thanks to your testimony, that's the fellow who's been locked up. Now supposing that were a member of my family—'

His cheek on the pillow, Audiat murmured:

'Don't count on me!'

It was around four. Maigret sat down beside the bed, poured himself a glassful of rum and filled a pipe.

'We have plenty of time to chat,' he said. 'I've just looked at your papers. So far you only have four convictions and they're not serious: pickpocketing, fraud, accessory to the burglary of a villa—'

Audiat was pretending to be asleep.

'Only, if I've done my sums correctly, one more conviction and it's exile to the colonies for you. What do you think?'

'Let me sleep.'

'I'm not stopping you from going to sleep. But you

won't stop me from speaking. I know that your friends aren't home yet. Right now, they're arranging things so that tomorrow, if I report their registration number, a garage owner will swear that their car didn't leave his garage this evening.'

Audiat's swollen lips stretched in a blissful smile.

'Except that I'll tell you one thing: I'll get Cageot! Whenever I've made up my mind to get someone, I've nabbed them in the end. Now the day when Cageot is hauled in, you will be too, and no matter how much you protest—'

By five in the morning Maigret had drunk two glasses of rum and the air was blue with pipe smoke. Audiat had tossed and turned so many times that he had ended up sitting up in bed, his cheeks red and his eyes shining.

'Was it Cageot who planned last night's little surprise? Most likely, eh? Eugène couldn't have thought of that all by himself. And if that is the case, you must be aware that your boss has no qualms about getting rid of you.'

A resident kept awake by Maigret's monologue stamped on the floor. The room was so hot that Maigret had removed his waistcoat.

'Give me some rum.'

There was only one glass, the water beaker, and the two men took it in turns to drink from it, without realizing how much alcohol they were downing. Maigret kept harking back to the same subject.

'I'm not asking much from you. Simply admit that, immediately after Pepito's death, Cageot came to fetch you from the café.'

'I didn't know that Pepito was dead.'

'You see! So you were at the Tabac Fontaine, as you were last night, with Eugène and probably the little hotel owner too. Did Cageot come in?'

'No!'

'Well, he knocked on the window. You must have had a pre-arranged signal.'

'I'm not talking.'

At six, the sky grew light. Trams rumbled past on the riverbank and a tugboat siren let out a heartrending wail as if, during the night, it had lost its barges.

Maigret's face was nearly as red as Audiat's, his eyes nearly as bright. The rum bottle was empty.

'I'm going to tell you, as a friend, what's going to happen now that they know that you came here and we talked. They'll repeat the operation as soon as they can, and this time they won't miss you. If you talk, what do you risk? We'll keep you in prison for a few days, for your own safety. When we've got the whole bunch of them banged up, we'll let you go and that will be it.'

Audiat listened attentively. He was clearly not entirely opposed to the idea, for he murmured, as if to himself:

'In the state I'm in, I'm entitled to go to the infirmary.'

'Of course. And you know the infirmary at Fresnes. It's even better than a hospital.'

'Can you check whether my knee is swollen?'

Maigret obeyed, removing the dressing. The knee had swollen, and Audiat, who was terrified of disease, prodded it anxiously.

'Do you think they'll have to amputate my leg?'

'I promise you that it will heal within a fortnight. You just have a little water on the knee.'

'Oh!'

He gazed at the ceiling and lay still for a few minutes. An alarm clock rang in another room. From the corridors came the muffled tread of the valet arriving on duty, then, from the landing, the relentless swish of a brush polishing shoes.

'Have you decided?'

'I don't know.'

'Would you rather end up in court with Cageot?'

'I'd like a drink of water.'

He was doing it deliberately. He was not smiling, but Maigret could sense his delight at being waited on.

'This water's warm!'

Maigret did not protest. His braces dangling, he ambled over and did everything the injured man asked of him. The horizon turned pink. A ray of sunshine licked the window.

'Who's in charge of the investigation?'

'Inspector Amadieu and the examining magistrate Gastambide.'

'Are they decent men?'

'There's no one better.'

'Admit that I was nearly a goner! How did I get run over?'

'By the car's left wing.'

'Was Eugène at the wheel?'

'It was him. The fellow from Marseille was with him. Who is he?'

'A young guy who arrived three months ago. He was in Barcelona, but apparently there's nothing going on there.'

'Now look here, Audiat. There's no point playing cat and mouse any longer. I'm going to call a taxi. The two of us are going to go to Quai des Orfèvres. Amadieu will arrive at eight o'clock, and you're going to tell him your story.'

Maigret yawned, so exhausted that he could barely speak.

'You're not saying anything?'

'All right, let's go and see what happens.'

Maigret gave his face a quick wash, adjusted his clothes and had two breakfasts brought up.

'You see, in a situation like yours, there is only one place where you are safe. And that's in prison.'

'Amadieu, isn't he the tall one, always pale-faced, with a droopy moustache?'

'Yes.'

'I don't like the look of him!'

The rising sun made Maigret think of his little house in the Loire and the fishing rods waiting for him in the bottom of the boat. Perhaps it was because he was so tired, but, for a split second, he was tempted to drop the whole thing. He looked at Audiat with round eyes, as if he had forgotten what he was doing there, and ran his hand through his hair.

'How can I get dressed, my trousers are all torn?'

They called the valet, who found Audiat an old pair of trousers. Audiat limped, groaned and leaned on Maigret with all his weight. The taxi drove over the Pont-Neuf and it was a relief to breathe in the sharp morning air. An empty van pulled out of police HQ, where it had just deposited its cargo of prisoners.

'Will you be able to walk up the stairs?'

'Maybe. In any case, I don't want a stretcher!'

Their destination was in sight. Maigret's chest felt tight with impatience. The taxi pulled up outside number 36. Maigret paid the fare and called over the uniformed orderly to help him get Audiat out of the car.

The orderly was talking to a man with his back to the street who wheeled round on hearing Maigret's voice. It was Cageot, wearing a dark overcoat, his cheeks grey with a two-day stubble. Audiat didn't spot him until he was out of the taxi, as Cageot, without even looking at him, resumed his conversation with the officer.

No words were exchanged. Maigret supported Audiat, who pretended to be much more seriously injured than he was.

Once they had crossed the courtyard, he sank down on to the first stair, like a man whose strength has failed him. Then, looking up, he sniggered:

'Ha, ha! I had you, didn't I! I've got nothing to say. I don't know anything. But I didn't want to stay in your room. Do I know you? How can I be sure it wasn't you who pushed me in front of the car?'

Maigret clenched his fist but kept it thrust in his overcoat pocket, hard as a rock.

7.

Eugène arrived first, just before eleven o'clock. Although it was not yet spring, his clothes reflected the sunny weather. He wore a light-grey linen suit, so soft that with every movement his muscles rippled beneath the fabric. His hat was the same shade of grey, and his shoes of fine buckskin. And when he pushed open the glass door of the Police Judiciaire, a gentle fragrance wafted into the corridor.

This was not the first time he had set foot inside Quai des Orfèvres. He glanced to the right and to the left, like a regular visitor, still smoking his gold-tipped cigarette. The morning briefing was over. People were waiting gloomily outside the inspectors' offices.

Eugène went up to the clerk, greeting him by raising a finger to his hat.

'Say, my good man, I believe Inspector Amadieu is expecting me.'

'Take a seat.'

He sat down casually, crossed his legs, lit another cigarette and opened a newspaper at the racing section. His blue limousine seemed to be stretching in front of the gate. Maigret spotted it from a window and went down into the street to inspect the left wing, but there were no scratches on it.

A few hours earlier, he had entered Amadieu's office without removing his hat, his expression wary.

'I've brought in a man who knows the truth.'

'That's a matter for the examining magistrate!' Amadieu had replied, continuing to leaf through a pile of reports.

Then Maigret had knocked on the chief's door and had gathered at once that his visit was not welcome.

'Good morning, sir.'

'Good morning, Maigret.'

They were both equally ill at ease and needed few words to communicate.

'Chief, I've worked all night and I've come to ask you to arrange for three or four individuals to be brought in for questioning.'

'That's up to the examining magistrate,' objected the head of the Police Judiciaire.

'The examining magistrate won't get anything out of them. You know what I mean.'

Maigret knew he was a thorn in everyone's side and that they would have liked to tell him to go to hell, but still he persisted. He stood there for ages, his massive bulk hovering over the chief, blocking his line of vision. Eventually the chief gave in and phone calls were made from one office to another.

'Come in here for a moment, Amadieu!'

'Coming, chief.'

Words were exchanged.

'Our friend Maigret tells me that . . .'

At nine, Amadieu steeled himself to go over to

Gastambide's office via the back corridors of the Palais de Justice. When he returned twenty minutes later, he had in his pocket the necessary warrants to question Cageot, Audiat, the owner of the Tabac Fontaine, Eugène, the fellow from Marseille and the short deaf man.

Eugène was already in the building waiting to see Amadieu, and so was Audiat. Maigret had made him come upstairs, where, since early morning, he had been sitting scowling at the end of the corridor watching the police officers' comings and goings.

At 9.30, inspectors set off to round up the others, while Maigret, heavy with sleep, roamed the establishment to which he no longer belonged, sometimes pushing open a door, shaking the hand of a former colleague or emptying his pipe into the sawdust of one of the spittoons.

'How are you doing?'

'Fine!' he replied.

'They're furious, you know!' Lucas whispered.

'Who?'

'Amadieu . . . The chief . . .'

And Maigret waited, soaking up the atmosphere of the place that had been his home. Ensconced in a red velvet armchair, Eugène showed no sign of impatience. On catching sight of Maigret, he even gave a cheery half-smile. He was a good-looking fellow, high-spirited and brimming with confidence. He exuded health and a happy-go-lucky attitude through every pore, and his tiniest movements displayed an almost animal grace.

An inspector came in from outside and Maigret hurried over to him.

'Did you go to the garage?'

'Yes. The garage owner says that the car was in the garage all night and the night watchman confirms his statement.'

The answer was so predictable that Eugène, who must have overheard, did not even bother to smirk.

It was not long before Louis appeared, bleary-eyed, annoyance written all over his face.

'Detective Chief Inspector Amadieu!' he grunted at the office boy.

'Have a seat.'

Acting as if he didn't recognize Eugène, Louis sat down three metres from him, his hat on his knees.

Inspector Amadieu called Maigret in and once again they found themselves facing each other in the small office overlooking the Seine.

'Are your rogues here?'

'Not all of them.'

'Do you want to tell me exactly what questions you want me to ask them?'

The seemingly friendly and deferential little phrase sounded so innocent. But it was an affirmation of passive resistance. Amadieu knew as well as Maigret that it is impossible to determine in advance the questions that will be asked during an interrogation.

Nevertheless, Maigret dictated a number of questions for each witness. Amadieu took notes with the obedience of a secretary and with blatant satisfaction.

'Is that all?'

'That's all.'

'Shall we begin right away with the one called Audiat?'

Maigret shrugged to indicate that he was not bothered, and then Amadieu pressed a bell, issuing orders to the inspector who appeared. His secretary sat at the end of the desk, with his back to the light, while Maigret sat in the darkest corner.

'Have a seat, Audiat, and tell us what you were doing last night.'

'I wasn't doing anything.'

Even though he had the sun in his eyes, Audiat had spotted Maigret and managed to glower at him.

'Where were you at midnight?'

'I can't remember. I went to the cinema, then I had a drink in a bar in Rue Fontaine.'

Amadieu glanced at Maigret to signal:

'Don't worry. I'll take your notes into account.'

And, his pince-nez on his nose, he slowly read out:

'What are the names of the friends you met in this bar?'

The battle was lost before it had begun. The questioning had got off to a bad start. The inspector sounded as if he was trotting out a lesson. Audiat, sensing this, grew increasingly bold.

'I didn't meet up with any friends.'

'And you didn't even notice someone who is here in this room?'

Audiat turned to Maigret and jerked his head in his direction.

'That gentleman maybe. But I'm not sure. I didn't take any notice of him.'

'And then?'

'And then I left. The cinema gave me a headache, so I went for a stroll along the boulevards. As I was crossing the road, I was hit by a vehicle and I ended up sitting at the base of a tree, injured. That gentleman was there. He told me I'd been knocked down by a car. I asked him to take me home, but he refused and took me to a hotel room.'

A door had opened to admit the chief of the Police Judiciaire, who stood silently, leaning against the wall.

'What did you tell him?'

'Nothing at all. He's the one who did all the talking. He spoke of people I don't know and he wanted me to come here and state that they were friends of mine.'

A chubby blue pencil in his hand, Amadieu scribbled the occasional note on his blotting pad, while the secretary recorded the full statement.

'Excuse me!' broke in the chief. 'This is all very well. But tell us what you were doing at three in the morning on Boulevard de La Chapelle.'

'I had a headache.'

'I wouldn't try and be clever, if I were you. When you've got four convictions already—'

'Excuse me! For the first two, I was granted an amnesty. You're not allowed to mention them.'

Maigret merely watched and listened. He smoked his pipe, the smell filling the office while the smoke curled upwards in the sunshine.

'We'll see about that in a few minutes.'

Audiat was taken into a neighbouring room. Amadieu telephoned:

'Bring in Eugène Berniard.'

The latter entered, smiling and relaxed. He glanced quickly around the room to identify who was sitting where, and stubbed out his cigarette in the ashtray.

'What were you doing last night?' repeated Amadieu listlessly.

'Well, inspector, I had a toothache, so I had an early night. Why don't you ask the night watchman from the Hôtel Alsina?'

'What time did you go to bed?'

'Midnight.'

'And you didn't drop in to the Tabac Fontaine?'

'Where's that?'

'Just a moment! Do you know a certain Audiat?'

'What does he look like? One meets so many people in Montmartre!'

Maigret was finding it increasingly difficult to sit still.

'Bring in Audiat!' said Amadieu into the telephone.

Audiat and Eugène stared at each other with curiosity.

'Do you know each other?'

'Never seen him before!' grunted Eugène.

'Pleased to meet you!' joked Audiat.

They barely bothered to put on an act. Their eyes were laughing, belying their words.

'So you weren't playing *belote* together last night at the Tabac Fontaine?'

One stared wide-eyed, the other burst out laughing.

'I'm afraid you're mistaken, *monsieur l'inspecteur*.'

The fellow from Marseille had just arrived, and was brought in to face the other two. He held out his hand to Eugène.

'Do you know each other?'

'Of course! We were together.'

'Where?'

'At the Hôtel Alsina. Our rooms are next to each other.'

The chief of the Police Judiciaire signalled to Maigret to follow him.

They paced up and down one end of the corridor where Louis was still waiting, not far from Germain Cageot.

'What do you intend to do?' The chief shot his companion an anxious look.

'Is it true they tried to kill you?' he asked.

Maigret did not answer. Unfazed, Cageot watched him with the same irony as Audiat and Eugène.

'If only I could have questioned them myself,' Maigret sighed at length.

'You know that isn't possible. But we'll carry on with the face-to-face confrontations for as long as you wish.'

'Thank you, chief.'

Maigret knew that it would be pointless. The five men were in cahoots. They had taken precautions. And it wasn't the questions that Amadieu was asking in his lugubrious tone that would force them to confess.

'I don't know whether you are right or wrong,' the chief added.

They walked past Cageot, who got to his feet and greeted the head of the Police Judiciaire.

'Was it you who summoned me, sir?'

It was midday. Most of the inspectors had gone to lunch or were on an assignment. The long corridor was almost empty. Pausing outside his door, the chief shook Maigret's hand.

'What more can I say? All I can do is wish you the best of luck.'

He went to collect his coat and hat and headed for the stairs, shooting a parting glance at the office where the interrogation was still ongoing and giving Cageot a dirty look.

Maigret's nerves were on edge. Never had he felt so suffocated by a sense of helplessness. Sitting side by side, Cageot and Louis were patient and relaxed, both amused at his comings and goings.

From Amadieu's office came a calm murmur of voices. Questions and answers succeeded each other with no urgency. The inspector followed the plan outlined by Maigret as promised, but without adding anything, without taking any interest.

Philippe was in prison! Madame Maigret was waiting impatiently for the postman.

'Nice day, isn't it?' said Cageot suddenly to his neighbour Louis.

'Very nice day. There's an easterly wind, though,' replied the latter.

'Have you been summoned too?'

This was for Maigret's benefit, with the barefaced intention of making fun of him.

'Yes. I think they need some information from me.'

'Same here. Who called you?'

'A certain Amadieu.'

As Maigret brushed past him, Cageot half-opened his mouth in a snigger and suddenly there was a violent reflex, impossible to control. Maigret's hand had smashed into Cageot's cheek.

That was a blunder! But it was the result of a sleepless night, and a whole string of humiliations.

While Cageot was left stunned by the brutality of the attack, Louis jumped up and grabbed Maigret's arm.

'Are you mad?'

Were they about to fight in the corridors of the Police Judiciaire?

'What's going on here?'

It was Amadieu, who had just opened his door. On seeing the three breathless men, no one could fail to grasp the situation, but the detective chief inspector said calmly, as if he had no idea:

'Would you step this way, Cageot?'

Once again, the other witnesses had been taken into the neighbouring office.

'Have a seat.'

Maigret followed them in and stood against the door.

'I asked you to come in because I need you to identify certain individuals.'

Amadieu pressed a bell and Audiat was shown in.

'Do you know this man?'

Then Maigret stomped out, slamming the door and swearing loudly. He could have cried. This charade appalled him.

Audiat did not know Cageot. Cageot did not know Audiat! Neither of them knew Eugène! And so it would go on ad nauseam! As for Louis, he knew no one!

Amadieu, who was questioning them, scored a point with each new denial. Huh! So Maigret dared to disrupt his little habits! Huh! He was trying to teach him his job!

He would remain polite to the end, because he was well brought-up, unlike some! But time would tell!

Maigret descended the drab stairs, crossed the courtyard and walked past Eugène's powerful car.

The sun was shining on Paris, on the Seine, on the sparkling Pont-Neuf. The warm air abruptly turned chilly as soon as you stepped into a patch of shade.

In a quarter of an hour, or in an hour, the interrogations would be over. Eugène would slide behind the wheel, next to his friend from Marseille. Cageot would flag down a taxi. They would go their separate ways after exchanging winks.

'That damned fool Philippe.'

Maigret was talking to himself. His feet pounded the cobblestones. He didn't know where he was going. At one point, he had the impression that a woman he passed quickly looked away to avoid being recognized. He stopped and glimpsed Fernande, who hastened her step. A few metres further on, he caught up with her and grabbed her arm with unintended violence.

'Where are you off to?'

She looked alarmed, and did not answer.

'When did they release you?'

'Last night.'

He realized that the trust that had existed between them was ruined. Fernande was afraid of him. All she wanted was to be on her way again as soon as possible.

'Were you summoned?' he asked, glancing towards the buildings of the Police Judiciaire.

'No.'

This morning she was wearing a blue suit that made her

look like a respectable woman. Maigret was all the more impatient since he had no further reason to detain her.

'Why are you going there?'

He followed Fernande's gaze, lighting on Eugène's blue car.

He understood. He felt offended, a pang of jealousy.

'Do you know he tried to kill me last night?'

'Who?'

'Eugène.'

She almost said something, but bit her lip.

'What were you about to say?'

'Nothing.'

The sentry was watching them. Upstairs, behind the eighth window, Amadieu was still taking the witness statements cooked up by the five men. The car was parked outside, lithe and light as its owner, and Fernande, her face set, was waiting for the chance to make her escape.

'Do you think it was me who had you locked up?' Maigret pressed her.

She said nothing and looked away.

'Who told you that Eugène was here?' he persisted in vain.

She was in love! In love with Eugène, with whom she had slept to please Maigret!

'Too bad,' he grunted finally. 'Off you go, dear!'

He hoped that she would retrace her steps, but she hurried towards the car and stood by the door.

The only person left on the pavement was Maigret. He filled his pipe, but was unable to light it, having tamped down the tobacco too hard.

8.

As he crossed the lobby of his hotel, Maigret tensed when a woman rose from a wicker armchair and started walking towards him. She kissed him on both cheeks with a sad smile and clasped his hand, keeping it in hers.

'This is terrible,' she moaned. 'I got here this morning and I've been running around so much that I don't know whether I'm coming or going.'

Maigret looked at his sister-in-law, who had turned up from Alsace. He needed to adjust to the sight of her, such a contrast was she from the images of the last few days and the morning, from the unsavoury world in which he was immersed.

Philippe's mother looked like Madame Maigret, but there was something more provincial about her. She wasn't plump but cuddly; she had a rosy complexion and carefully smoothed hair, and everything about her exuded cleanliness – her black and white outfit, her eyes, her smile.

It was the atmosphere of the countryside that she brought with her and Maigret thought he caught a whiff of her house, with its cupboards filled with home-made jam, the aroma of the little delicacies and desserts which she loved cooking.

'Do you think he'll be able to find a job after all this?'

Maigret picked up his sister-in-law's luggage, which was even more provincial than she was.

'Are you staying here?' he asked.

'If it's not too expensive . . .'

He showed her into the dining room, where he never set foot when he was alone, for it had an austere atmosphere and people only spoke in whispers.

'How did you get hold of my address?'

'I went to the Palais de Justice and I saw the examining magistrate. He wasn't aware that you were handling the case.'

Maigret said nothing but pulled a face. He could hear his sister-in-law's voice imploring: *You understand, sir. My son's uncle, Divisional Chief Inspector Maigret—*

'Then what?' he asked irritably.

'He gave me the address of the lawyer in Rue de Grenelle. I went there too.'

'You did all that carrying your suitcases?'

'I put them in left-luggage.'

It was astounding. She must have told the whole world her story.

'I tell you, when the photograph appeared in the newspaper, Émile didn't dare go to his office!'

Émile was her husband. Philippe had inherited his myopic squint.

'In our part of the world, it's not like Paris. Prison is prison. People say that there's no smoke without fire. Does he at least have a proper bed with blankets?'

They ate sardines and rounds of beetroot, and drank a carafe of table wine. From time to time Maigret made an effort to steer the conversation away from the obsessive topic of Philippe.

'You know Émile. He's very angry with you. He blames you. He says it's your fault that Philippe joined the police instead of looking for a good job in a bank. I told him that whatever will be, will be. By the way, how's my sister? Not finding the animals too much work?'

Luncheon lasted a good hour, for afterwards they had to have a coffee and Philippe's mother wanted to know exactly how a prison is built and how the prisoners are treated. They were in the lounge when the doorman came to inform them that a gentleman wished to speak to Maigret.

'Show him in!'

He wondered who it could be and was more than astonished to see Inspector Amadieu, who greeted Madame Lauer awkwardly.

'Philippe's mother,' said Maigret.

And, to the detective chief inspector:

'Shall we go up to my room?'

They went upstairs in silence. Once inside the room, the inspector cleared his throat and put down his hat and the umbrella which never left his side.

'I thought I'd see you after the interrogation this morning,' he began. 'But you left without saying a word.'

Maigret watched him without speaking. He knew that Amadieu had come to make peace, but was not gallant enough to make things easier for him.

'Those boys are very good, you know! I realized it when they were brought face to face with each other.'

He sat down to give an impression of composure, and crossed his legs.

'Look, Maigret, I've come to tell you that I'm beginning to share your opinion. You see that I'm being honest with you and that I bear no ill will.'

But his voice did not sound entirely natural and Maigret sensed that this was a lesson learned and that Amadieu had not taken this step of his own accord. After that morning's interrogations, there had been a meeting between the chief of the Police Judiciaire and Amadieu, and it was the chief who had been in favour of Maigret's theory.

'Now, I'm asking you: what should we do?' said Amadieu solemnly.

'I have no idea!'

'Don't you need my men?'

Then, suddenly garrulous:

'I'll tell you what I believe. Because I thought long and hard while I was questioning those rogues. You know that when Pepito was killed, he'd been issued with a summons. We knew that there was a rather large drugs cache at the Floria. And it was to stop them from moving the drugs that I had posted an inspector there until the arrest, which was planned for dawn. Well, the stuff has vanished.'

Maigret appeared not to be listening.

'From that, I deduce that when we lay our hands on it we'll have the murderer too. I've a good mind to ask the magistrate for a search warrant and to pay a visit to our friend Cageot.'

'There's no point,' sighed Maigret. 'The man who masterminded this morning's face-to-face confrontation wouldn't have kept such a compromising package in his home. The stuff isn't at Cageot's, or Eugène's, nor at the homes of any of the others. By the way, what did Louis have to say about his customers?'

'He swears he's never seen Eugène, even less played cards with him. He thinks Audiat might have come in a few times to buy cigarettes, but he has never spoken to him. As for Cageot, while the name rings a bell, like everyone in Montmartre, he didn't know him personally.'

'And they didn't slip up, naturally?'

'Not once. They even exchanged amused looks as if the interrogation was a farce. The chief was furious.'

Maigret found it hard to repress a little smile, for Amadieu had admitted that his hunch was correct and that his own change of heart was thanks to the head of the Police Judiciaire.

'We could always have an inspector tail Cageot,' continued Amadieu, who found silences awkward. 'But he'll have no trouble shaking him off. Not to mention that he has protection and that he's capable of filing a complaint against us.'

Maigret pulled out his watch, which he gazed at insistently.

'Do you have an appointment?'

'Shortly, yes. If you don't mind, we'll go downstairs together.'

As they passed the doorman, Maigret inquired after his sister-in-law.

'The lady left a few minutes ago. She asked me which bus she should take to get to Rue Fontaine.'

That was typical! She wanted to see for herself the place where her son was accused of having killed Pepito. And she would go inside! She'd tell her story to the waiters!

'Shall we have a drink at the Chope on the way?' suggested Maigret.

They sat down in a corner and ordered a vintage Armagnac.

'You have to admit,' ventured Amadieu, tugging at his moustache, 'that your method is impossible to apply in a case like this one. The chief and I were arguing about it earlier.'

Well, well, the chief really was taking a close interest in the case!

'What do you mean by my method?'

'You know better than I do. Usually, you get involved in people's lives; you try to understand their thinking and you take as much interest in things that happened to them twenty years earlier as you do in concrete clues. Here, we're faced with a bunch about whom we know pretty much everything. They don't even try to put us off the scent. And I'm not even sure that, in private, Cageot would even bother to deny having killed.'

'He hasn't denied it.'

'So what do you plan to do?'

'What about you?'

'I'll start by spreading a net around them, that's the best thing. From this evening, I'll have each one of them followed. They'll have to go somewhere, talk to people. We'll question those people and—'

'And in six months' time Philippe will still be in prison.'

'His lawyer intends to request his interim release. As he is only accused of manslaughter, he's bound to obtain it.'

Maigret could no longer feel his tiredness.

'Another?' suggested Amadieu, pointing to the glasses.

'With pleasure.'

Poor Amadieu! How uncomfortable he must have felt when he walked into the hotel lounge! By now, he'd had the time to regain his composure and adopt a deceptive air of confidence, and even to speak of the case with a certain casualness.

'As a matter of fact,' he added, taking a sip of Armagnac, 'I wonder whether Cageot is actually the killer. I've been mulling over your hypothesis. Why wouldn't he have given Audiat the job of shooting? He himself could have been hiding in the street—'

'Audiat would never have retraced his steps to bump into my nephew and raise the alarm. He'd be likely to lose his bottle. He's a nasty little thug but small fry.'

'What about Eugène?'

Maigret shrugged, not because he believed Eugène to be innocent, but because he would have found it awkward to implicate him. It was very vague. Fernande had something to do with it.

Besides, Maigret was barely in the conversation. His pencil in his hand, he was doodling aimlessly on the marble table top. The room was hot. The Armagnac produced a mellow feeling of well-being, as if all his accumulated fatigue were gradually dissipating.

Lucas came in with a young inspector and gave a start on seeing Maigret and Amadieu sitting side by side. Maigret winked at him across the room.

'Why don't you come over to HQ?' suggested Amadieu. 'I'll show you the transcript of the interrogations.'

'What's the use?'

'What do you intend to do?'

He was on edge. What could be brewing behind Maigret's stubborn brow? Already he was being slightly less cordial.

'We mustn't let our efforts undermine each other. The chief is of the same opinion as me and it's he who advised me to reach an agreement with you.'

'Well, aren't we agreed?'

'About what?'

'About the fact that Cageot killed Pepito and that it was probably he who killed Barnabé a fortnight earlier.'

'Being agreed about it isn't sufficient grounds to arrest him.'

'Of course not.'

'So?'

'So nothing. Or rather, I will only ask one thing of you. I imagine it will be easy for you to get a summons against Cageot from Gastambide?'

'And then what?'

'Then I'd like there to be an inspector on duty at Quai des Orfèvres with that summons in his pocket. As soon as I telephone him, he should come and meet me.'

'Meet you where?'

'Wherever I am! It would be better if instead of one summons, he has several. You never know.'

Amadieu's glum face had grown longer.

'Fine,' he snapped. 'I'll talk to the chief.'

He called the waiter and paid for one round. Then he spent ages buttoning and unbuttoning his overcoat in the hope that Maigret would finally say something.

'Well! I wish you every success.'

'That's very kind. Thank you.'

'When do you think it will be?'

'Perhaps later today. Perhaps not until tomorrow morning. Actually, I think it would be better if it were to happen tomorrow morning.'

Just as his companion was heading off, Maigret had an afterthought.

'And thank you for coming!'

'You're welcome.'

Left on his own, Maigret paid for the second round, then paused at the table where Lucas and his colleague were sitting.

'Any news, chief?' asked Lucas.

'Soon. Where will I be able to get hold of you at around eight tomorrow morning?'

'I'll be at Quai des Orfèvres. Unless you'd rather I came here.'

'See you tomorrow here!'

Outside, Maigret stopped a taxi and asked to be dropped off in Rue Fontaine. Night was falling. Lights went on in the windows. As they drove past the Tabac Fontaine, he asked the driver to slow down.

In the little bar, the dozy girl was at the till, the owner behind the bar, while the waiter was wiping the tables. But there was no sign of Audiat, or Eugène or his friend from Marseille.

'I bet they're furious at being deprived of their game of *belote* this evening!'

A few moments later, the taxi drew up opposite the

Floria. Maigret asked the driver to wait, and pushed the half-open door.

It was cleaning time. A single lamp was on, casting a wan light over the wall hangings and the red and green paintwork. The tablecloths had not yet been put on the unvarnished tables, and the musicians' instruments lay scattered around the stage still in their cases.

The overall effect was shabby and dismal. The office door, at the back, was open and Maigret had a fleeting glimpse of a woman's shape. He walked past a waiter sweeping the floor and suddenly emerged into the bright light.

'It's you!' exclaimed his sister-in-law.

Her face was flushed and she became flummoxed.

'I wanted to see the—'

A young man was leaning against the wall, smoking a cigarette. It was Monsieur Henry, the Floria's new owner, or rather Cageot's new front man.

'This gentleman has been very kind—' stammered Madame Lauer.

'I wish I could have done more,' apologized the young man. 'Madame has told me that she's the mother of the police officer who killed . . . I mean who's accused of shooting Pepito. I know nothing about it. I took over the place the following day.'

'Thank you again, monsieur. I can see that you understand what it's like to be a mother.'

She was expecting Maigret to read her the riot act. Once they were in the waiting taxi, she talked for the sake of talking.

'You came by car? There's a very good bus . . . I don't mind if you smoke your pipe . . . I'm used to it . . .'

Maigret gave the address of the hotel, then, on the way, he murmured in a strange voice:

'This is what we're going to do. We've got a long night ahead of us. Tomorrow morning, we must be fresh, our nerves steady and our minds alert. We can go to the theatre, how about that?'

'To the theatre, while poor Philippe's in prison?'

'Bah! This will be his last night.'

'Have you found out something?'

'Not yet. Let me do as I see fit. The hotel is depressing. There's nothing for us to do there.'

'And I was wanting to take this opportunity to go and tidy Philippe's room!'

'He would be furious. A young man doesn't want his mother going through his things.'

'Do you think that Philippe has a young lady?'

All her provincialism was distilled in these words. Maigret kissed her on the cheek.

'Of course not, silly goose! Sadly he hasn't. Philippe is a real chip off the old block.'

'I'm not certain that before Émile married me he—'

It was like bathing in clear water. When they arrived at the hotel, Maigret booked seats at the Palais-Royal theatre, then, before dinner, he wrote a letter to his wife. He appeared to have forgotten all about Pepito's murder and his nephew's arrest.

'You and I are going to paint the town red!' he told his

sister-in-law. 'If you're a good girl, I'll even show you the Floria in full swing.'

'I'm not dressed for that!'

He kept his word. After an elegant dinner in a restaurant on one of the Grands Boulevards – because he didn't want to eat at the hotel – he took his sister-in-law to the theatre and enjoyed watching her laugh at the bedroom farce despite herself.

'I feel bad at what you're making me do,' she sighed during the interval. 'If Philippe were to know where his mother was right now!'

'And what about Émile! I hope he's not whispering sweet nothings to the maid.'

'She's fifty, poor thing.'

It was harder to get her to agree to set foot in the Floria. She was already overwhelmed by the neon lights in the entrance to the nightclub. Maigret steered her towards a table by the bar, brushing against Fernande, who was there with Eugène and his sidekick from Marseille.

As one might expect, there were smiles at the sight of the good woman being piloted by the former detective inspector.

And Maigret was thrilled! It was as if that was what he had been hoping for! Like a decent provincial fellow out for a good time, he ordered champagne.

'I'll be tipsy!' simpered Madame Lauer.

'Good!'

'Do you realize this is the first time I've set foot in a place like this?'

She really was a babe in the woods! She was a paragon of moral and physical virtue!

'Who's that woman who keeps staring at you?'

'That's Fernande, a friend of mine.'

'If I were in my sister's shoes, I'd be worried. She looks lovesick.'

It was true and yet it wasn't. Fernande had been making eyes at Maigret, as if she rued losing the intimacy that had been disrupted. But she immediately clutched Eugène's arm and made an exaggerated show of flirting with him.

'She's with a very handsome young man!'

'The sad thing is that tomorrow the handsome young man will be in prison.'

'What did he do?'

'He's one of the gangsters who got Philippe arrested.'

'Him?'

She couldn't believe it. And it was worse when Cageot poked his head through the curtain to see how things were going, as he did every night.

'You see that gentleman who looks like a lawyer?'

'With the grey hair?'

'Yes! Well, be careful. Try not to scream. He's the murderer.'

Maigret's eyes were laughing as if he already had Cageot and the others at his mercy. Then he was laughing out loud so hard that Fernande turned round in surprise and frowned, anxious and wistful all of a sudden.

A little later, she made her way to the toilets, glancing at Maigret as she walked past. He stood up to go and talk to her.

'Have you got any news?' she asked, almost spitefully.

'What about you?'

'Nothing. As you can see, we're having a night out.'

She watched Maigret closely and said after a silence:

'Is he going to be arrested?'

'Not straight away.'

She stamped her high-heeled foot on the floor.

'The love of your life?'

But she was already marching off.

'Don't know yet,' she retorted.

Madame Lauer was ashamed to be going to bed at two in the morning, while Maigret fell into a deep sleep as soon as his head touched his pillow, snoring as he had not done for a few days.

9.

At 7.50, Maigret dropped in to the hotel office just as the owner, who had just arrived, was reviewing the guest list with the night watchman. A bucket of dirty water stood in the middle of the corridor; there was a broom leaning up against the wall and Maigret, with the utmost serious-ness, grabbed the broom and examined the handle.

'May I use this?' he asked the owner, who stammered: 'Feel free . . .'

Then he had second thoughts and asked anxiously:

'Is your room not clean enough?'

Maigret was smoking his first pipe of the day with unmitigated pleasure.

'My room is fine!' he replied, unperturbed. 'It's not the broom I'm interested in. I'd just like a little piece of the handle.'

The cleaning woman, who had appeared and was wiping her hands on her blue apron, must have thought he had gone mad.

'You wouldn't have a little saw, would you?' Maigret asked the night watchman.

'Go on, Joseph,' the owner said, 'go and fetch a saw for Monsieur Maigret.'

Thus the fateful day began on a comic note. It was another sunny morning. A chambermaid entered with a breakfast tray. The floor of the corridor had just been washed down. The postman came in and rummaged in his leather satchel.

Maigret, broom in hand, was waiting for a saw.

'There is a telephone in the lounge, I believe?' he asked the owner.

'Yes, there is, Monsieur Maigret. On the table to your left. I'll connect you right away.'

'There's no need.'

'Don't you want to make a call?'

'No thank you. It's not necessary.'

He entered the lounge with his broom, while the cleaning woman declared:

'I'd just like to say that it's not my fault I'm standing here twiddling my thumbs. You'd better not yell at me for not finishing the lobby!'

The night watchman returned with a rusty saw, which he had found in the basement. Meanwhile, Maigret reappeared with the broom, took the saw from him and began sawing off the end of the handle. He rested the broom on the desk. Sawdust fell on to the newly washed floor. The other end of the handle rubbed against the register while the owner looked on in dismay.

'There! Thank you very much,' said Maigret at length picking up the small round of wood which he had just sawn off and handing back the broom minus a few centimetres to the cleaning woman.

'Is that what you needed?' asked the hotel owner, keeping a straight face.

'Exactly.'

At the Chope du Pont-Neuf, where he met up with

Lucas in the back room, cleaners and their buckets were everywhere, as at the hotel.

'You know that the squad worked all night, chief. When Amadieu left you, he got it into his head to beat you to it, and put everyone on the case. I even know that you went to the Palais-Royal theatre with a lady.'

'And then that I went to the Floria? Poor Amadieu! What about the others?'

'Eugène was at the Floria too. I expect you saw him. At 2.45 he left with a tart.'

'Fernande, I know. I bet he slept at her place in Rue Blanche.'

'You're right. He even left his car parked outside all night. It's still there.'

Maigret had raised an eyebrow, even though he wasn't in love. The other morning, it was he who had been in her sun-drenched apartment. Fernande had sat there half naked drinking her *café au lait* and there had been an intimate sense of trust between them.

It wasn't jealousy, but he was not very fond of men like Eugène, whom he could picture now, still in bed, while Fernande fussed around making coffee and bringing it to him. What a condescending smile he must have on his lips!

'He'll get her to do anything he wants,' he sighed. 'Go on, Lucas.'

'The Marseille sidekick hung around a couple of clubs and then went back to the Hôtel Alsina. He'll be asleep at this hour because he never rises before eleven or midday.'

'What about the little deaf man?'

'His name is Colin. He lives with his wife – turns out he

is lawfully married – in an apartment in Rue Caulaincourt. She makes a scene when he comes home late. She used to be the madam in his brothel.'

'What's he doing right now?'

'He's at the market. He's the one who always does the shopping, wearing a long scarf around his neck and carpet slippers on his feet.'

'Audiat?'

'He went on a bar crawl and got drunk as a lord. He returned to his hotel in Rue Lepic at around one in the morning and the night watchman had to help him up the stairs.'

'And Cageot's at home, I imagine?'

On coming out of the Chope du Pont-Neuf, Maigret had the impression he could see his characters dotted around the Sacré-Cœur, whose white dome emerged from the Paris mist.

For ten minutes he issued instructions to Lucas in an undertone, murmuring as he shook his hand:

'Is everything clear? Are you sure you don't need more than half an hour?'

'Are you armed, chief?'

Maigret patted his trouser pocket and hailed a passing taxi.

'Rue des Batignolles!'

The door of the concierge's lodge was open and the gas-man was standing in the doorway.

'Can I help you?' asked a voice with a northern accent as Maigret walked past.

'Monsieur Cageot, please.'

'On the mezzanine, to the left.'

Maigret paused on the threadbare doormat to get his breath back. He yanked the heavy silk cord, which set off a soft tinkling inside the apartment, sounding like a child's toy.

Here too a broom was sweeping the floor, occasionally hitting a piece of furniture. A woman's voice said:

'Are you going to open the door?'

Then there was the sound of muffled footsteps. A chain was taken off. A key turned in the lock and the door opened, but barely ten centimetres.

It was Cageot who had opened the door. He was in his dressing gown, his hair tousled, his eyebrows bushier than ever. He was not surprised. He looked Maigret in the eye and snarled:

'What do you want?'

'First of all, to come in.'

'Are you here officially, with a proper warrant?'

'No.'

Cageot wanted to shut the door again, but Maigret had wedged his foot in the gap so it wouldn't close.

'Do you not think it would be better if we talked?' he said.

Cageot realized that he wouldn't be able to close his door and his expression darkened.

'I could call the police—'

'Of course! Except that I think that it wouldn't do you any good and that a conversation between just the two of us would be preferable.'

Behind Cageot, a cleaning woman dressed in black had stopped work to listen. All the doors were open for her to clean the whole apartment. Leading off the corridor to the left Maigret had the impression there was a light-filled room overlooking the street.

'Come in.'

Cageot locked the door again, put the chain on and said to his visitor:

'To the right . . . in my office . . .'

It was a typical lower-middle-class Montmartre apartment, with a kitchen barely one metre wide looking on to the courtyard, a bamboo coat-stand in the hall, a gloomy dining room with gloomy curtains and wallpaper with a faded leaf pattern.

Cageot's 'office' had been designed to be the sitting room and was the only room in the apartment to have two windows letting in the light.

A polished wooden floor. In the centre were a worn rug and three upholstered armchairs that had taken on the same indefinable hue as the rug.

The walls were dark red, cluttered with a large number of paintings and photographs in gilt frames. And in the corners pedestal tables and shelves were laden with worthless knick-knacks.

A mahogany desk with an old morocco top stood near one of the windows. Cageot chose to seat himself behind it, tidying away some papers that had been lying carelessly on the right-hand side.

'Marthe! Bring me my hot chocolate in here.'

He did not look at Maigret. He waited, preferring to let his visitor launch the offensive.

Meanwhile, Maigret, sitting on a chair that was too spindly for his burly frame, had unbuttoned his overcoat and filled a pipe, tamping the tobacco down with his thumb, staring about him as he did so. A window was open, probably to air the place, and when the cleaning woman arrived with the hot chocolate Maigret asked Cageot:

'Do you mind if we shut the window? I caught a chill yesterday and I don't want to make my cold worse.'

'Close the window, Marthe.'

Marthe had taken a dislike to the visitor. It was clear from the way she busied herself around him, banging into his leg in passing and making no apology.

The room was filled with the smell of chocolate. Cageot cupped the bowl in his hands as if to warm them. Outside in the street, delivery lorries drove past, their roofs reaching almost to the windows, as did the omnibuses' metallic tops.

Marthe went out, leaving the door ajar, and continued cleaning the hall.

'I won't offer you a hot chocolate,' said Cageot, 'as I imagine that you have had your breakfast.'

'I have, yes. But if you had a glass of white wine—'

Everything mattered, every single word, and Cageot frowned, wondering why his visitor was asking for a drink.

Maigret understood, and smiled.

'I'm used to working outdoors. In winter, it's cold. In summer, it's hot. In both cases, a man needs a drink—'

'Marthe, bring some white wine and a glass.'

'Everyday wine?'

'That's right. I prefer everyday wine,' replied Maigret.

His bowler hat sat on the desk, next to the telephone. Cageot sipped his chocolate without taking his eyes off Maigret.

He was paler in the morning than in the evening, or rather his skin was drained of colour, his eyes the same dull grey as his hair and eyebrows. He had an elongated, bony face. Cageot was one of those men who it is impossible to imagine anything other than middle-aged. It was hard to believe that he had ever been a baby, or a schoolboy, or even a young man in love. He could never have held a woman in his arms and whispered loving words to her.

On the other hand, his hairy hands, which were nicely manicured, had always wielded a pen. The desk drawers must have been full of papers of all kinds – accounts, calculations, bills and memoranda.

'You're up relatively early,' commented Maigret after glancing at his watch.

'I don't sleep more than three hours a night.'

He was speaking the truth. It was hard to say how you could tell, but you could.

'So, do you read?'

'I read, or I work.'

They granted each other a moment's respite. There seemed to be a tacit understanding that the real conversation would begin once Marthe had brought in the white wine.

Maigret couldn't see a book case, but on a small table by the desk were some bound books: the penal code, Dalloz law manuals, legal tomes.

'Leave us, Marthe,' said Cageot as soon as the wine was on the table.

As she reached the kitchen, he nearly called her back to tell her to close the door, but changed his mind.

'I'll leave you to pour it yourself.'

Meanwhile, as if it were the most natural thing in the world, he opened a desk drawer and took out an automatic revolver, which he placed within reach. It did not even feel like a provocation. He was acting as though this were completely normal behaviour. Then he pushed away the empty bowl and rested his elbows on the arms of his chair.

'I'm ready to hear your proposal,' he said, with the air of a businessman meeting a client.

'What makes you think that I have a proposal to put to you?'

'Why else would you be here? You are no longer a member of the police, so you haven't come to arrest me. You can't be here to question me since you are no longer a sworn officer, and anything you say afterwards will be of no consequence.'

Maigret assented with a smile as he relit his pipe, which he had allowed to go out.

'On the other hand, your nephew is up to his neck in trouble and you can't see any way of getting him off.'

Maigret had put his box of matches on the brim of his hat and had to reach for it three times in quick succession, because the tobacco, which was probably packed too tightly, kept going out.

'So,' concluded Cageot, 'you need me but I don't need you. Well, I'm all ears.'

His voice was quite neutral, as colourless as his persona. With his face and a voice like that, he would have made a tremendous criminal judge.

'Fair enough!' decided Maigret, rising and taking a few

steps. 'What would you want in exchange for getting my nephew off the hook?'

'Me? What can I do?'

Maigret smiled pleasantly.

'Come, don't be modest. It's always possible to undo what one has done. How much?'

Cageot remained silent for a moment, digesting this offer.

'I'm not interested,' he said at length.

'Why not?'

'Because I have no reason to help this young man. He deserves to go to prison for what he did. I don't know him.'

Maigret paused from time to time in front of a portrait, or in front of the windows, looking down into the street, where housewives jostled each other around little market barrows.

'For example,' he muttered softly, lighting his pipe yet again, 'if my nephew were exonerated, I would no longer have the slightest reason to involve myself in this case. You said so yourself, I am no longer a member of the police force. To be honest with you, I confess I'd jump on to the first train to Orléans and two hours later I'd be in my little boat, fishing.'

'You're not drinking!'

Maigret poured himself a full glass of white wine, which he drained in one gulp.

'As for what you can do,' he went on, sitting down and putting the matchbox back on the brim of his hat, 'there are a number of options. When the witnesses are brought face to face for the second time, Audiat could be less certain of his recollection and not formally identify Philippe. That happens all the time.'

Cageot grew pensive and, seeing his absent look, Maigret guessed that he was not listening, or barely paying attention. But no! He must have been asking himself:

'Why the devil has he come to see me?'

And from then on, Maigret's chief concern was to avoid looking in the direction of the hat and the telephone at all costs. It was also vital that he appear to mean what he said. Whereas in fact, he was wasting his breath. To loosen his tongue he filled another glass and drank it.

'Is it good?'

'The wine? Not bad. I know what you're going to say. If Philippe is exonerated, the investigation will be re-opened all the more energetically, since there will no longer be a culprit.'

Cageot looked up imperceptibly, curious as to what was to come. Maigret suddenly turned red as a thought struck him.

What would happen if, at the same moment, Eugène, or his friend from Marseille, or the owner of the Tabac Fontaine or anyone were to try to reach Cageot on the telephone? It was possible, probable even. The previous day, the entire gang had been hauled in to Quai des Orfèvres and they must all be feeling somewhat anxious. Wasn't Cageot in the habit of giving orders and receiving reports over the telephone?

But, for the time being, the telephone was out of action, and it would remain so for a few long minutes more, perhaps for an hour.

Maigret had put his hat down on the desk in such a way

as to conceal the base of the telephone from Cageot's view. And each time he picked up the box of matches, he slid the little round of wood he had sawn off that morning under the receiver.

In other words, the call had begun. Lucas was stationed at the telephone exchange with two shorthand typists who would take everything down.

'I understand that you're lacking a culprit,' muttered Maigret staring at the rug.

What would happen if Eugène were to try to telephone Cageot and fail to get through was that he would come running. Maigret would be back to square one! Or rather it would be impossible to start again since Cageot would be on his guard.

'It's not difficult,' he went on, trying to keep a steady voice. 'You just need to find some boy who is of roughly the same build as my nephew. There's no shortage in Montmartre. And there must be one whom you wouldn't mind seeing locked up. Two or three testimonies into the bargain and it's in the bag.'

Maigret was so warm that he removed his overcoat and hung it over the back of a chair.

'May I?'

'We could open one of the windows,' suggested Cageot.

Oh no! With the noise from the street, the shorthand typists on the other end of the line wouldn't be able to hear half of the things that were said.

'Thank you, but it's my influenza that's making me sweat. The cold air would do me more harm. I was saying—'

He drained his glass and filled a fresh pipe.

'I hope the smoke doesn't bother you?'

They could still hear Marthe bustling around, but sometimes the noise stopped and she must have been eavesdropping.

'Just give me a figure. What's the price for an operation like that?'

'Jail!' retorted Cageot, bluntly.

Maigret smiled, but he was beginning to doubt his strategy.

'In that case, if you're afraid, suggest another scheme.'

'I don't need a scheme! The police have arrested a man they allege killed Pepito. That's their business. True, from time to time, I do a small favour for the Ministry of the Interior or for the police. As it happens, I know nothing. I wish for your sake that I did—'

He made as if to get up to put an end to the conversation. Maigret needed to think fast.

'Shall I tell you what's going to happen?' he enunciated slowly.

He took his time, speaking syllable by syllable:

'In the next two days, you will have to kill your little friend Audiat.'

The message struck home, that was certain. Cageot avoided looking at Maigret, who continued, for fear of losing his advantage:

'You know it as well as I do! Audiat is a kid. Furthermore, I suspect him of taking drugs, which makes him impressionable. Since he's been aware that I'm on to him, he has made one blunder after another, panicked and, the other night, in my room, he actually came clean. It was very clever of you to be waiting for us outside the Police

Judiciaire to stop him from repeating what he'd told me. But you might not be so lucky another time. Last night, Audiat went on a bar crawl and got drunk. He'll do the same tonight. There'll be someone tailing him all the time.'

Cageot sat absolutely still, his eyes fixed on the dark-red wall.

'Go on,' he said in a perfectly normal voice.

'Do I have to? How will you go about eliminating a man under police surveillance day and night? If you don't kill him, Audiat will squeal, that's for certain! And if you kill him, then you'll be caught, because it's difficult to commit a murder under those conditions.'

The ray of sunshine filtering through the grimy window slid over the desk and, in a few minutes, would reach the telephone. Maigret smoked his pipe taking rapid little puffs.

'What do you have to say to that?'

Without raising his voice, Cageot said:

'Marthe! Shut the door.'

She did so, grumbling. Then he lowered his voice, speaking so softly that Maigret wondered whether his words would carry down the telephone.

'And supposing Audiat were already dead?'

He didn't bat an eyelid as he said this. Maigret remembered his conversation with Lucas, in the Chope du Pont-Neuf. Hadn't the sergeant stated that Audiat, followed by an inspector, had gone back to his hotel in Rue Lepic, at around one o'clock in the morning? And the inspector must have kept a watch on the hotel for the rest of the night.

His hand resting on the worn leather desk top, a few centimetres from the revolver, Cageot went on:

'You see that your offer doesn't stand up. I thought you were better than that.'

And, as Maigret froze with dread, he added:

'If you want to know more, you can telephone the police station of the 18th *arrondissement*.'

As he spoke these words, he could have reached for the receiver and handed it to Maigret. But he didn't, and Maigret breathed again, saying hastily:

'I believe you. But I haven't quite finished yet.'

He didn't know what he was going to say. But he had to play for time. At all costs, he had to get Cageot to say certain words which he seemed to be avoiding like the plague.

So far, he had not once denied the murder. But nor had he said a single word that could be considered as a formal confession.

Maigret imagined Lucas growing impatient, the earpiece pressed to his ear, poor Lucas veering from hope to despair and saying to the typists:

'There's no need to type that.'

What if Eugène or someone else called?

'Are you sure that what you have to tell me is worth it?' persisted Cageot. 'It's time for me to get dressed.'

'Please give me another six minutes.'

Maigret poured himself a drink and rose like a very nervous man about to launch into a speech.

10.

Cageot did not smoke, did not move, had no nervous twitches that could provide an outlet for his jumpiness.

Maigret had not yet realized that it was precisely this stillness that bothered him, but it dawned on him when he saw Cageot reach out towards a comfit box that was on the desk, and help himself to a sugared almond.

It was a small detail, and yet Maigret's eyes lit up as if he had discovered the chink in Cageot's armour. The man was neither a smoker nor a drinker nor a womanizer, but he liked sweets, sucking a sugared almond and passing it slowly from one side of his mouth to the other!

'I could say that we are among professionals here,' said Maigret at length. 'And it's as a fellow professional that I'm going to tell you why, inevitably, you'll be caught.'

The sugared almond in his mouth moved faster.

'Let's take the first murder. I'm talking about the first murder in this series, because it is possible that you have others to your name. Wasn't the solicitor to whom you were chief clerk poisoned?'

'It was never proved,' said Cageot simply.

He was trying to work out what Maigret was leading up to. At the same time, Maigret's mind was working overtime.

'It doesn't matter! It's now three weeks since you decided

to eliminate Barnabé. As far as I can tell, Barnabé was the link between Paris and Marseille, in other words, between you and the Turks who bring the drugs in by boat. I'm guessing that Barnabé wanted to take too big a cut. He was invited to get into a car at night. Suddenly, Barnabé feels a knife stabbing him in the back and a few moments later his body is thrown out on to the pavement. You see the error?'

Maigret picked up his matches to ensure that the round of wood was still in place. At the same time, he wanted to conceal a faint smile that he was finding hard to suppress, for Cageot was thinking, earnestly trying to spot the mistake like a diligent schoolboy.

'I'll tell you later,' promised Maigret, interrupting his train of thought. 'For the time being, I'll go on. The police, through some coincidence, are on to Pepito. Since the stuff is at the Floria and the Floria is being watched, the situation is dangerous. Pepito knows he's going to get caught. He threatens to squeal if you don't save him. You shoot him with a revolver at a time when he thinks he's alone in the empty club. Here, no mistakes.'

Cageot looked up and the sugared almond remained poised on his tongue.

'No mistakes so far. Are you beginning to follow me? But you realize there is a police officer inside the club. You exit. You can't resist the urge to get the police officer arrested. At first, it seems like a stroke of genius. And yet, that was the mistake, your second.'

Maigret was on the right track. All he needed to do was go on, without rushing things. Cageot listened and mulled things over while anxiety was beginning to gnaw away at his composure.

'Third murder, that of Audiat. Audiat too was about to talk. The police are watching him. The knife and the gun are out. I bet Audiat was in the habit of having a drink of water during the night. This time, he'll drink even more because he is drunk, and he won't wake up because the water in the jug has been poisoned. Third mistake.'

Maigret staked his all, but he was sure of himself! Things couldn't have happened any other way.

'I'm waiting to hear what the three mistakes were!' said Cageot after a moment, reaching for the box of sugared almonds.

And Maigret imagined the hotel in Rue Lepic, whose residents were mainly musicians, gigolos and prostitutes.

'In the Audiat case, the mistake is that someone put the poison in the jug!'

Cageot was baffled, sucked another sugared almond, and there was a faintly sweet smell in the air, a hint of vanilla.

'With Barnabé,' continued Maigret pouring himself a drink, 'you took at least two people with you: Pepito and the driver, probably Eugène. And it was Pepito who subsequently threatened to squeal.

'Are you with me? Result: the need to eliminate Pepito. You were only dealing with the shooting. But you added the extra touch of going to fetch Audiat, whose job was to bump into the inspector. What automatically happens? Eugène, Louis, the owner of the Tabac Fontaine, a *belote* player called Colin and Audiat are now in the know. It is

Audiat who loses his nerve. And so you have to get rid of him!

'But, yesterday afternoon, you didn't go to Rue Lepic yourself. You must have used a resident at the hotel whom you contacted by telephone. Another accomplice! A man who might talk! Are you with me now?'

Cageot was still ruminating. The sun reached the nickel-plated telephone receiver. It was late. A crowd was swelling around the little barrows and the clamour from the street could be heard in the apartment despite the closed windows.

'You're good, that's clear. But then, why do you keep lumbering yourself with useless accomplices who are likely to give you away? You could have easily bumped off Barnabé at any time, he wasn't suspicious of you. You didn't need Audiat in the Pepito business. And yesterday, when you weren't under surveillance, you could have gone to Rue Lepic yourself. In these hotels, where there's no doorman, anyone can just walk straight in.'

Occasionally footsteps could be heard on the stairs, and Maigret had to force himself to appear calm and carry on talking as if nothing were amiss.

'Right now, there are five people at least who can have you put away. Now, five people have never managed to keep a secret like that for long.'

'I didn't stab Barnabé,' said Cageot slowly. He was gloomier than ever.

Maigret jumped at the opportunity and stated confidently:

'I know!'

Cageot looked at him in surprise and narrowed his eyes.

'A stabbing is more up the street of an Italian, like Pepito.'

He needed to make one more tiny effort, but just then the cleaning woman opened the door and Maigret thought his edifice was going to collapse.

'I'm off to the market,' she announced. 'What vegetables shall I get?'

'Whatever you like.'

'Can you give me some money?'

Cageot took two ten-franc coins from a sturdy, well-worn purse with a metal clasp, a real miser's purse. The wine bottle on the table was empty and he held it out to Marthe.

'Here! You can get the deposit back on this. You have the receipt.'

His mind was elsewhere, however. Marthe left without shutting the door, but she did close the kitchen door behind her and water could be heard boiling on the stove.

Maigret had been watching Cageot's every move, and forgotten about the telephone and the typists lying in wait on the other end of the line. He had a sudden intuition, he couldn't have said exactly when. He had talked a lot, without thinking too hard about what he was saying, and now he was within a hair's breadth of the truth.

Added to which were the sugared almonds in the comfit box, the purse and even the word 'vegetable'.

'I bet you're on a diet.'

'It's been twenty years.'

Cageot was no longer talking about throwing his visitor out. It even seemed as if he needed him. Seeing Maigret's empty glass, he said:

131

'Marthe will bring some more wine. There's never more than one bottle in the house.'

'I know.'

'How do you know?'

Because it fitted in with all the rest, of course! Because now, for Maigret, Cageot had stopped being an adversary and had become a man. And he knew this man better with each second. He felt him live, breathe, think, fear and hope. He could hear the irritating rattle of the sugared almond against his teeth.

The decor came to life too – the desk, the furniture, the paintings, as cloying as jam.

'Do you know what I think, Cageot?'

These were not just hollow words, but the culmination of a long chain of thought.

'I'm asking myself if you really did kill Pepito. Right now, I'm almost certain you didn't.'

His tone had changed. Maigret was fired up, leaning forwards to get a closer look at Cageot.

'I'm going to tell you straight away why I think that. If you had been capable of shooting Pepito yourself, you wouldn't have needed anyone to kill Barnabé and Audiat. The truth is that you're afraid.'

Cageot's lips were dry. Even so he attempted an ironic smile.

'Just you dare to tell me that you have slaughtered a chicken or a rabbit! Dare to tell me that you are capable of seeing blood flow from a wound!'

Maigret no longer had any doubts. He had understood. He charged ahead.

'Let's get this straight. You are afraid to kill with your own hands, but you have no compunction about doing away with a person! On the contrary! You are afraid of killing, afraid of dying. But that makes you all the more determined to order murders. Isn't that true, Cageot?'

Maigret's voice was devoid of hatred, devoid of pity. He studied Cageot with the fascination with which he studied human beings in general. And this man was terribly human in his eyes. Nothing had been left to chance, not even his first job as a solicitor's clerk.

Cageot was and always had been completely withdrawn. All alone, his eyes closed, he must dream up brilliant schemes, schemes of all kinds, financial, criminal and erotic.

Had he ever been seen with women? Of course not! Women were not capable of enacting his wild fantasies!

Cageot retreated into himself, into a lair filled with his thoughts, his dreams, his smell.

And when he looked out of his windows at the street below bathed in sunlight, where people teemed around the market stalls and packed buses rumbled past, what he was inclined to do was not to mingle with the living mass of humanity outside, but to use it as inspiration for his cunning schemes.

'You are a coward, Cageot!' thundered Maigret. 'A coward like all those who live only by their brains. You sell women, cocaine, and God only knows what else – for I believe you are capable of anything. But at the same time you are a police informer!'

Cageot did not take his grey eyes off Maigret, who was unstoppable.

'You had Barnabé killed by Pepito. And I'm going to tell you who you had kill Pepito. In your gang, there is a good-looking young man, who has everything going for him – women, money and success. He's happy-go-lucky and completely devoid of a conscience.

'Just you dare to tell me that the night of Pepito's murder you weren't at the Tabac Fontaine! There was the owner, then that brothel-owner Colin, who is even more of a coward than you, then Audiat, the fellow from Marseille and lastly Eugène.

'It was Eugène whom you sent to the Floria. Then, when he came back, having done the job, and told you there had been someone inside the club, you brought Audiat in.'

'And then what?' said Cageot. 'What use is all this to you?'

He gripped the arms of his chair with both hands as if he wanted to get up. He thrust his head slightly forwards, in a movement of defiance.

'What use is it to me? To prove to you that I'll get you, precisely because you are a coward and you have surrounded yourself with too many people.'

'I swear you won't ever get me.'

He had a mirthless smile. His pupils had contracted. He added slowly:

'The police have never been very clever! Earlier you mentioned poisoning. Seeing as you were once in the police, you can probably tell me how many poisonings they expose every year in Paris?'

Maigret did not have time to reply.

'Every year! You hear me? You can't be naive enough to believe that out of a population of four million, there aren't a few who succumb to an overdose of arsenic or strychnine?'

He got to his feet at last. Maigret had been expecting him to do this for some time. It was the release after too long an effort, and the release inevitably expressed itself in words.

'I could have killed you today. I thought about it. All I needed to do was poison your wine. You'll note that the bottle is already gone from the house. All I'd need to do is rinse your glass. You'd leave here and you'd go and die somewhere—'

Maigret had a doubt, but it lasted only a fraction of a second.

'You are right. I didn't kill Barnabé. I didn't kill Pepito. I didn't even kill that idiot Audiat!'

Cageot, comfit box in hand, spoke softly and continuously. He was a ridiculous sight with his dressing gown that was too short and his unkempt hair giving him a strange halo. Had it not been for the telephone, Maigret would have opened a window to escape this oppressive atmosphere of a reclusive existence.

'What I say to you is of no consequence, since you are not a sworn police officer and there are no witnesses.'

As if overcome by doubt, he glanced at the corridor and even opened the door to his bedroom for a moment.

'The thing you have not understood, you see, is that they won't betray me, even if they want to, because legally they are guiltier than I am! Eugène has killed. It's Louis who supplied the gun and the key to the Floria. And do you know what might happen if Eugène tried to be clever? Little Monsieur Colin, as you call him, that half-deaf little runt with a stutter, has instructions to slip something in his glass one night while they're playing *belote*. I promise you, in this game, it's not as necessary as you might think to be capable of slitting a chicken's throat.'

Maigret had gone over to the desk to pick up his hat and his matches. His knees were trembling slightly. It was over. He had achieved his goal. All he had to do was to get out. The inspector waiting outside in the street had a summons in his pocket. At Quai des Orfèvres they were waiting for news and were probably laying bets on the outcome.

Maigret had been there for two hours. Eugène, in silk pyjamas, was perhaps having a late breakfast with Fernande. And where on earth might Philippe's dear mother be?

There were footsteps on the stairs, followed by a violent knocking on the apartment door. Cageot looked Maigret in the eyes, then gazed at his revolver, which was still lying on the desk.

While he went to open the door, Maigret put his hand on his gun pocket and stood stock-still in the middle of the room.

'What's going on?' came Eugène's voice from the hall.

The two men were instantly at the door to the office. There were more footsteps behind them, those of Fernande, who stared at Maigret in surprise.

'What the—?' repeated Eugène.

But already a car was pulling up outside with a squeal of brakes.

Eugène ran to a window.

'I knew it!' he groaned.

The police, who had been watching Fernande's place and had followed the couple, jumped out on to the pavement.

Cageot didn't budge. His revolver in his hand, he was thinking.

'Why have you come here?'

He was addressing Eugène, who was talking at the same time.

'I telephoned four times and—'

Maigret had inched backwards so as to have his back to the wall.

At that, Cageot glanced at the telephone. Just then a shot rang out, the room was filled with the smell of burnt gunpowder and a bluish cloud hung in the sunlight.

Maigret had fired. The bullet had hit Cageot's hand, causing him to drop the revolver.

'Don't move!' said Maigret, who was still pointing his gun.

Cageot stood rooted to the spot. In his mouth he still had a sugared almond, which made his left cheek bulge. He did not dare move a muscle.

There were footsteps on the stairs.

'Go and open the door, Fernande,' commanded Maigret.

She sought Eugène with her eyes to know whether she should obey, but her lover was staring stubbornly at the floor. So she walked resignedly across the hall, undid the chain and unlocked the door.

Blood was dripping from Cageot's hand, plopping on to the rug, where a brownish stain was spreading.

Suddenly, before Maigret could do anything, Eugène made a dash for one of the windows, flung it open, breaking a pane, and jumped out.

Screams rose up from the street. Eugène had landed on the roof of a stationary car, leaped to the ground and started running in the direction of Rue des Dames.

At that moment, two inspectors appeared in the doorway.

'What's going on?' they asked Maigret.

'Nothing. You are going to arrest Cageot, against whom there is a summons. Have you got back-up downstairs?'

'No.'

Fernande had no idea what was happening. She stood gazing at the open window in a stupor.

'Then he'll run for a long time!'

As he spoke, Maigret picked up the round of wood and slipped it into his pocket. He had the feeling that something was afoot with Cageot, but it wasn't serious. Cageot had crumpled to the floor and rolled on the rug, where he lay inert.

He had fainted, probably at the sight of his blood splashing on to the rug, drop by drop.

'Wait till he comes round. Call a doctor if you must. The telephone is working now.'

Maigret shoved Fernande on to the landing and made her go down the stairs ahead of him. A crowd had gathered in front of the building. A beat sergeant was trying to fight his way through it.

Maigret elbowed his way out of the crush and he and Fernande found themselves outside the charcuterie on the corner of the street.

'The love of your life?' he asked.

Then he noticed that she was wearing a new fur coat. He felt it.

'Did he give it to you?'

'Yes, this morning.'

'By the way, do you know that he's the one who killed Pepito?'

'Oh!'

She hadn't batted an eyelid. He smiled.

'Did he tell you?'

She merely fluttered her eyelashes.

'When?'

'This morning.'

And she added, suddenly solemn, like a woman in love who believes it's the real thing:

'You won't get him!'

And she was right. A month later, she went to join Eugène in Istanbul, where he had opened a nightclub on the famous Grand Rue de Pera.

As for Cageot, he was a book-keeper in prison.

Madame Lauer wrote to her sister:

I'm sending you by express delivery six plum tree saplings like the ones we have in the garden at La Tourelle, as you requested. I think they'll take very well in the Loire. But you should tell your husband that in my view he doesn't prune his fruit trees properly, he should take off more branches.

Philippe is much better since he's been back home. He's a good boy who barely ever goes out and loves doing crosswords in the

evening. But in the last few days, I've seen him hanging around
the Scheffers' house (the owners of the gasworks) and I think
there are wedding bells in the air.

   Tell your husband too that last night they put on the play
that we saw together at the Palais-Royal. But it didn't go down
as well as it did in Paris . . .

Maigret came in wearing his waders and holding three
pike at arm's length.

'But we're not going to eat those, are we?' said his wife.

'Of course not!'

He said that in such an odd tone of voice that she raised
her head to look at him. But no! He was already going into
the shed to put away his fishing rods and take off his boots.

'If we had to eat everything we killed!'

The words formed in his mind of their own accord at
the same time as a ridiculous image, that of an
ashen, perplexed Cageot confronted with the bodies of
Pepito and Audiat. It did not even bring a smile to his face.

'What soup have you made?' he shouted, sitting down
on a crate.

'Tomato.'

'Good!'

And the rubber boots fell to the beaten earth floor one
after the other as he heaved a contented sigh.